D*o I detect a* note of Christmas cynicism in my guest?" Peter asked her.

Kim-ly Geneviève Beauchamp stopped in place, halfway to the White House, as if her feet had just frozen to the ground. Lit warmly by the soft lights, she stood amid the fluttering snow that graced her hair like momentary stars.

The Secret Service flowed smoothly around them. Within moments they were as good as standing alone. The agents circled about them, facing outward.

"No, Mr. President," she looked directly at him for the first time.

Somehow, Peter had forgotten her eyes. Golden skin, elegant features, and rich brown hair that flowed down gloriously, practically to her elbows, were what drew your attention if you had even a hint of a Y-chromosome. But it was her green eyes that appeared to hide nothing that were her most startling feature.

"You misinterpret. I'm never a cynic about Christmas. You detect a note of caution because I don't know what you want from me, Mr. President. I am the UNESCO Chief of Unit for Southeast Asia World Heritage Sites. I am not political, I am *specifically* not political. So, therefore I am cautious, as I do not understand why I am here at the lighting of your National Christmas Tree."

The Night Stalkers

Peter's Christmas

by

M. L. Buchman

Buchman Bookworks

Discover more by this author at: www.buchmanbookworks.com

Cover images:
MH-60L DAP Direct Action Penetrator Blackhawk Helicopter
© Adam Pflum
White House and the National Christmas Tree
© Robert Crow | Dreamstime.com
Man and Woman Couple In Romantic Embrace On Beach
© Darren Baker | Dreamstime.com
Red and green candy cane over white
© Lucie Lang| Dreamstime.com (back cover)

Other works by this author:

<u>**M.L. Buchman**</u>

The Night Stalkers
The Night Is Mine
I Own the Dawn
Daniel's Christmas
Wait Until Dark
Frank's Independence Day
Peter's Christmas
Take Over at Midnight

...

Angelo's Hearth
Where Dreams are Born
Where Dreams Reside
Maria's Christmas Table

...

Swap Out!

<u>**Matthew Lieber Buchman**</u>

Nara
The Nara Threshold
The Nara Effect

Second Dark Ages
Monk's Maze

Dieties Anonymous
Cookbook from Hell: Reheated
Saviors 101: the first book of the reluctant Messiah

Dedication

To my fans.
Without you, I'd be writing in the Dark
rather than in the Light.

Chapter 1

It was December first and Kim-Ly Geneviève Beauchamp of Vietnam stood not twenty paces from the base of the American National Christmas Tree on Washington, D.C.'s Ellipse. The slight fluttering of snow was captured in the streetlights of the park, enchanting for the news cameras, making the scene glitter like a fairyland. Her breath made small white clouds that softened the night even more.

She had come to the lighting of the tree every year that her UNESCO job placed her in D.C. or even New York at the right time of year. Something about this moment—the colors, the children filled with wonder, the spectacular music, the President's message—had always filled her with a hope and a joy. It reminded her of so many good things in the world. She also attended the lighting of the New York tree in Rockefeller Center whenever she could. Though her tropical blood was never thick enough to convince her to join in ice skating with the holiday crowds who made it look so fun.

"*Tu es un* Christmas sap *absolu*, Genny," her mother often accused her with a gentle smile; their family language a crazy mix of French heritage and Vietnamese homeland, overlaid with the ubiquitous English. And her mother was absolutely correct. She was.

But this year was different. Genny wasn't shoulder to shoulder with mothers and children and small business owners and twenty

1

thousand others who had braved the cold and dark of a D.C. winter night. She wasn't blocked from a clear view of the tree by the fifty reporters, their cameras, and their lights.

This year she stood close beside cabinet members, White House staffers, and soon, the United States President and his phalanx of Secret Service guards who would be arriving at the podium for the lighting of the tree.

"What am I doing here?"

"At the President's personal invitation," a Secret Service agent standing beside her whispered back in response.

"Oh sorry," she turned to face the female agent who looked neat and dangerous in her suit and long overcoat, with the telltale coil of wire leading up to her ear mostly hidden by dark hair. "I was actually speaking to myself. I do that."

"No worries, ma'am," the agent didn't look the least put out or the least worried that she might have offended. "Always takes a bit of getting used to, your first trip to the White House."

Of course, the Secret Service would know that about her. She wondered what else the agent knew about her life now that Genny was the President's personal guest to the tree lighting ceremony. Did the woman know that five months earlier Genny had practically hijacked a meeting at the U.N. to convince the President to pay more attention to the UNESCO World Heritage Sites in Southeast Asia? That had been one of her most audacious acts, irritating the Vietnamese, Laotian, and Cambodian U.N. ambassadors in the process. Or that she'd since dodged three invitations to the White House prior to this one?

The towering tree was still unlit. A U.S. Marine Corps Band was playing *Good King Wenceslas*. And who would follow in this good President's steps through the winter that seemed to chill the news headlines? She shook off the thought as being unworthy of a Christmas moment.

Most of the White House staffers were talking to each other as earnestly as if they were still inside their warm offices. A few of them had joined in singing carols with the crowd. She tried to sing along as she normally would, knowing she had a passable, if French-accented soprano, but she couldn't even seem to mouth the words in a throat gone dry.

Some delay in the proceedings left her too much opportunity to wonder quite why she had avoided the invitations before, though two out of three times she'd been legitimately flying out of the country the next day.

So, why had she accepted this one? Because she'd be in Washington anyway for the tree lighting, though the President had no way to know that. And she'd been surprised. The call hadn't come from some staffer as before, it had come from President of the United States Peter Matthews himself. She'd recognized his voice immediately despite only meeting him the one time. Though she'd certainly watched enough of his speeches since then, far more than could be justified by her passing interest in American politics. He'd charmed her into coming, made her deny that she'd been avoiding him, even though she had. And she wasn't sure why she'd been doing that either.

She liked the President the one time they'd met. Enjoyed his sharp mind and insightful questions. Through the U.S. Ambassador to the U.N., she'd begun receiving an uncharacteristic degree of cooperation. The United States had assisted her several times now with information and gentle political pressure. So, she'd decided her efforts had been successful and left it at that. She'd soon moved on to other avenues, to leverage her goals to protect Heritage Sites from desperate governments teetering on the edge of open conflict.

America's relationship with the U.N., and by extension UNESCO, had always been a little dicey anyway and she didn't see it as her mission to fix that. That would be far above her mandate, though the outstanding billion-plus dollars in arrears would have helped so much. Geneviève didn't expect more than had already been given. The Americans' interest in Southeast Asia had always been tinged with a combination of benign neglect for the present and deep-seated uneasiness based on the collective memories of the Vietnam War and what they'd perpetrated both in Vietnam and in the surrounding countries.

She had turned down the car that the White House had offered and taken the train down as usual. Then spent the three hours in transit worrying instead of enjoying the ride as she usually did. Agent Beatrice Ann Belfour had attached herself to Genny at the front gate, her guide and guard. That perhaps was partly to protect Genny, and partly to protect against her, regarding the President.

"Heads up, incoming," Agent Belfour whispered to her privately.

She was about to ask what she meant, then realized she already knew, and steeled herself. Sure enough. At the end of the tale of the good king trudging through the snow to feed a poor but worthy man, the President of the United States strode down the lawn from the White House.

The Marine Corps Band broke into *Hail to the Chief.*

President Matthews, still immensely popular despite this being near the end of his second year in office, practically leapt onto the platform and called into the microphone for them to hush. He did it with a laugh and a smile that was easy for the crowd and even the band members to join in.

She found that she too was laughing despite herself. He exuded energy and hope with that simple gesture. Was it natural or calculated? She'd butted heads with enough politicians over the years to assume the latter, but it didn't feel that way. It felt as if he meant everything he did.

He was tall and trim. His hair drifted down to his collar, befitting for the youngest President in history. His brown eyes sought hers, a smile lit his face as he spotted her among the crowd. He was also terribly handsome and clearly knew it. Before she could even think to respond in kind, he had turned away and then shouted to the crowd, "Merry Christmas, America!"

The crowd, obviously enamored of their leader, shouted back in near unison, "Merry Christmas, Mr. President!"

"Is he always like this?" Geneviève whispered to the agent.

"No, sometimes he's worse. At least according to my husband." She nodded to the massive agent who hovered close beside the President without appearing to. If Agent Belfour looked dangerous, the head of the Presidential Protection Detail looked lethal.

"What do you do when you're not riding herd on some guest?"

"Oh, odd jobs." Belfour's simple evasion spoke volumes to Genny.

She rarely needed security herself, did her best to avoid it even if she really should have it in tow. She'd found that negotiations were much easier at World Heritage Sites if you weren't totting along a personal militia. Even when the local warlords were, perhaps especially then. Still, she'd worked with security escorts enough to know that the really good ones played down their roles.

#

"So, Kim-Ly, did you enjoy the speech?" Peter knew it was a lame opening, but he didn't know how else to start off. The tree was lit, the crowd had cheered, and America had been given both a colorful display and a happy Christmas message. Now, clear of the reporters and their cameras, his nerves had set in.

He'd managed to time his placement in the crowd for the five-minute walk back to the White House so that he'd be beside her through the Presidential Park. It would have been too much to have her walk with him down to the tree lighting, so he'd come up with them meeting at the tree itself as a comfortable place to begin. But now he didn't know where to start.

"Geneviève. Only my Vietnamese grandmother calls me Kim-Ly as I was named for her."

Okay, so she went by her middle name. He'd missed that somewhere.

He'd refused to let the Secret Service tell him anything more about her after that first meeting at the U.N. He didn't want to take any advantage of his Presidential powers in this. Let the Secret Service do what was necessary to approve her for security, but keep it to themselves. It actually placed him at a disadvantage, as his own life was so public. But entering politics had been his choice, or maybe his first wife's choice, but that didn't mean it was Geneviève's choice. Her name was a bit of a mouthful but it had a long elegance, much as she did.

After they crossed over the closed 'E' Street, they entered the Presidential Park by the Southwest Gate. They were in the lead, a dozen agents ranged about them, and the rest of the staff followed behind chattering among themselves. The waist-high concrete wall could stop a large truck and the spike iron fence mounted atop it kept all but the most suicidal out of the grounds. They crossed the lawn past the tennis and basketball courts, presently covered with a light sheen of snow.

She looked at him, as if she were peering around the corner made by the thick fall of mahogany hair beside her cheek. Hair that reached to the middle of her back. Her features were poised and aristocratic. Her skin reflected her mixed French and Vietnamese heritage—European aristocratic features, almond-shaped eyes, and golden skin. She looked splendid and exotic. But he recalled that it had been her passion in her beliefs that had captivated him at the United Nations building in New York last July. Though her stunning looks hadn't hurt.

"As for your speech, it has its purpose served."

"Ha. Well, that puts me in my place, doesn't it?" Peter tried not to feel put out, but he did, no matter how childish the thought. "The speechwriters wanted a meatier speech, but I wanted to—"

"Keep it short, upbeat, and make people focus less on worry and more on good cheer." Her voice was like a fifth player in a string quintet. Once you were used to the sound of four instruments, then a second viola begins to play, offering new and unique insights into the music the four others had been creating.

"Uh, yes. That's exactly what I was trying for." Not a single thing was missed by his guest's sharp mind. Those had been his own guide-words for himself as he wrote it.

"Then, it has its purpose served."

"Is that Ms. Geneviève Beauchamp's form of high praise?" Was he so desperate for approval? For that, he could have talked to any of the dozen or more staffers and that many again service agents who accompanied him along the walkways back to the White House. No, it was *her* approval he seemed to be begging for. He'd convinced himself that it merely reflected a desire to engage and welcome her, but he did want her to like him.

"Staying and singing *O Christmas Tree* was a nice touch. I'm sure it played well to the public."

"Do I detect a note of Christmas cynicism in my guest?"

She stopped in place, halfway to the White House, as if her feet had just frozen to the ground. Geneviève, lit warmly by the soft lights, stood amid the fluttering snow that graced her hair like momentary stars.

The Secret Service flowed smoothly around them. Within moments they were as good as standing alone. The agents circled about them, facing outward. The rest of the staffers continued on their way to warmer climes and hot coffee indoors.

"No," she looked directly at him for the first time since last July.

Somehow, Peter had forgotten her eyes. Golden skin, elegant features, and rich brown hair that flowed down gloriously, practically to her elbows, were what drew your attention if you had even a hint of a Y-chromosome. But it was her green eyes that appeared to hide nothing that were her most startling feature.

"You misinterpret. I'm never a cynic about Christmas. You detect a note of caution because I don't know what you want from me, Mr. President. I am the UNESCO Chief of Unit for Southeast Asia World Heritage Sites. I am not political, I am *specifically* not political. So, therefore I am cautious, as I do not understand why I am here."

He smiled. He'd asked himself that exact same question. What had he been hoping for when he invited her. The fragment of an answer he'd come up with had influenced how he'd altered tonight's speech.

"You are here because I truly enjoyed meeting you and I wanted to see you again. I'm only sorry it didn't happen sooner."

She studied him for several long moments, her expression unreadable. He remembered that from their meeting at the U.N. This was a woman in absolute control of her own emotions. Not to mention her facial expressions.

"And that is all that you are intending?" She didn't radiate the doubt she must be feeling. She made it sound as if it were a simple question.

Peter nodded, "That's all. That encompasses the vast extent of my nefarious hidden agenda."

"Ah. I understand now, Mr. President," her soft smile appeared for the first time since he'd lit the tree.

Peter always loved watching the crowd in that brilliant moment when he lit the National Christmas Tree. That shared held breath when the decorations were lit and the year's design was revealed to the nation. He had worked with the designer and they'd created a red-and-white spiral of thirteen wide bands that swooped upward to a star-studded blue top, with a traditional golden star at the pinnacle. They'd overlapped the red and white strings between each stripe, wiring them into something called a "chase" unit, which caused the lines to shift slightly about the tree. The tree looked like a flag unfurling in the breeze.

No ornaments other than the fifty "stars" in the field of blue, each a shining image of the fifty states' official mammals. If the news agencies didn't catch onto that bit of whimsy in a day or so, the designer would tip someone off. His personal favorite was the Maine Moose with the Washington State Orca coming a close second.

But tonight Peter had watched only Kim-Ly Geneviève Beauchamp of Vietnam as he pressed the button that lit the tree. She had become glorious in that moment. Her smile radiating as brightly as the kajillion Christmas lights.

"If that is indeed the entire scope of your plan, Mr. President, what you should do is offer me a gentleman's escort. Then perhaps we can start this conversation once again." She made it sound as simple as that.

So he took her at her word and held out his arm for her. She slipped a hand about his elbow. He could feel her touch as if her thin red leather glove and his thick wool coat didn't exist.

She turned with him and they and their circle of protectors progressed once more along the frosty roadway toward the main entrance to the Residence.

"Where did I begin our conversation?" Peter was distracted by her simple touch.

"With the speech."

"Ah," he tried to think of a better opening, but had little luck finding one. "That was a lame beginning."

"It was, but the speech served its purpose."

He did his best to suppress a groan, but didn't succeed well. This was an improvement? Frank, the head of his Presidential Protection Detail turned to check that he was okay. Geneviève must have heard it, but she didn't react. Rather, she continued talking as if he had made no interruption.

"It served its purpose in that it has made me glad that I accepted your invitation."

It was a high compliment indeed. Peter had no response to it. He had again totally misread her meaning, which was very unusual for him. His gift was reading what people wanted, both as individuals and in groups. He'd then address everyone in their own worldview semantics in order to build agreement and accord. Yet, he'd misread her twice in under a minute. How had she done that to him?

"Now," she pointed across the South Lawn. "Tell me how you make this fountain work when any water with the least common sense would be now frozen." Her French juxtaposition of the verb made her sound even more charming.

He watched the central jet splash merrily despite their frosty breath and the snowflakes swirling gently down out of the winter's night sky.

"Maybe it thinks warm thoughts? I have no idea."

# # #

Genny had always wanted to see the inside of the White House, especially at Christmas. From the outside there were no great displays, no grand dressing of decorations. Perhaps, it was the woman's role to decorate the White House. But the First Lady had died in that tragic helicopter accident two years ago, not even spending an entire year in the White House. Katherine Matthews had never had a chance to decorate a single Christmas. That was a great sadness, on top of all the others.

Still, Genny would be terribly disappointed if she found it wasn't decorated on her first, and probably only, visit here.

It had been sweet of the President to invite her. But even if she were to trust that he had no ulterior motive, what possible reason could she have to be involved in any way with such a man? The American-proclaimed "Leader of the Free World" had much to answer for in many places. Though she had been pleasantly surprised that this one did not believe that a sound foreign policy was in direct conflict with a sound domestic one. So many of his predecessors had done just that.

They walked along the driveway that circled the South Lawn. Clearly uncomfortable, she let him play guide by pointing out the Putting Green, which he never used, the Swimming Pool, which he often used, though he noted that he did that only in warmer weather, and several trees which even she knew he named completely wrong, but the effort was rather cute.

The first glimmer of Christmas decoration hope came when she saw the two sweeping stairways leading up to the broad porch of the South Portico. White twinkle lights adorned the stair's handrails and the porch's stone balustrade. It was a delicate statement on such a massive structure but it cheered her nonetheless.

His attempts to play guide wholly collapsed as they climbed the steps. He clearly knew less about the building's history than the grounds. He huffed out a great cloud of frustrated breath, then spoke quickly, waving an arm to encompass the entire structure.

"It was designed by aliens. The whole place. George and Martha Washington were pod people. Probably Dolly Madison too, though not James. At least according to the super-secret Area 51 files that the FBI did *not* give to me the day I was elected."

"And what *did* they give you?" The frustrated rant had been the most human thing she'd heard from the man. It was the first time Genny wondered if perhaps he had spoken truth, and really had no political motive for inviting her.

"Frankly, they gave me a headache. It was a very disillusioning day. Do you know how many identified troublespots there are on this planet and how many of those are right in our country?"

"This is not my country, Mr. President."

"Right, sorry. Of course it isn't. Sorry. I really must learn to keep my mouth shut."

They climbed up the Portico's stairs in awkward silence for several moments. She finally could take it no longer and attempted to rescue him.

"The snow is so pretty. It was good of you to arrange that." It would give him a chance to say, "Did it just for you." Then she could dismiss the easy flattery and the man along with it. It was touching that he had been thinking of her when he'd altered his speech. Against expectation, he slowed and stared up at the fluttering flakes until a few began to accumulate on his cheeks and forehead for a brief moment before melting.

"Snow? I'd guessed that they were tiny crystalline alien spaceships, still cold from the depths of outer space, come to take back the White House that George built."

Genny looked away to face the building so that he wouldn't see her expression. She didn't want him to know that he had confused her.

Most men had one of two reactions to her, three actually.

One, they assumed she'd made her career with her beauty and discounted her mind totally. A view they rarely maintained after even a single meeting in which they did not agree with her.

Two, they saw her as a target for the bastioning of their male egos, because of course they could easily conquer her. All of the men with this type of response, she had gladly disillusioned. Only two had required a brief personal demonstration of her self-defense training to permanently convince them.

The third type simply became tongue-tied around her which she never really understood, she had a mirror after all and knew she wasn't nearly that level of extraordinary. But she had learned early on how to read and use all three reactions to her advantage. Genny occasionally felt guilty for doing this but, as she only used it to save precious Heritage Sites and not on her own behalf, she didn't feel too guilty.

With President of the United States Peter Matthews, she had apparently found a fourth response. Her presence did not stun him to silence nor fill him with avarice nor knot up his tongue, but it certainly did fluster him. Again the word "cute" came to mind, but she rather doubted that he'd appreciate the observation, so she kept it to herself.

He also provided a wit and humor that he didn't reveal to the nation. Charm? Yes. Quirky humor? Not that she had observed. He had more dimensions than Genny had anticipated.

He led her up to the center of the Portico. They paused at the balcony rail. The South Lawn was spread before them, and off in the distance, the patriotic swirl of flag-colored lights climbed the glowing three-story tall tree. Beyond it, the brilliant needle of the Washington Monument soared into the night sky, clearly stating, "Here lies the source of America's power. Here is rooted her mighty spear."

"Terribly phallic, no?" She teased.

"Maybe the Founding Fathers had an inferiority complex."

He made it easy for her to laugh. "They did but you do not?"

"Not until I met you." In the soft light of the Portico, Genny could see that he actually blushed. "Did I really just say that out loud?"

"Indeed you did." Nor was she likely to forget it. While he wasn't the first man she'd smitten, he was the first who was so honest about it.

"Come," he cleared his throat. "There is something I think you will enjoy before we go up to the Residence for a small gathering."

As he turned her by her hand still in the crook of his arm, she spotted the Secret Service agents, hers, his, and two others standing by the wall. The President did not appear flustered by their presence, so she did her best to not be as well. She'd felt alone with him for a moment, and been enjoying that feeling. Her attempts to hold onto that failed under the four agents' roving gazes. Though they didn't look at her, it was clear they were completely aware of her every move.

He led her to what appeared to be a large window in the center of the rounded wall behind the Portico that was the great signature bay of the White House. At some signal she didn't see, two of the agents raised up the window sash until it was higher than her head. Then reaching down, they opened a pair of waist-high double doors. It was like a secret passage through a window and into an unknown world. She and the President were able to walk through the door or window or whatever it was and into…

Her breath caught in her throat. A stunning tree of massive proportions filled the center of the room. The room was oval, but she was pretty sure the Oval Office wasn't located in the Residence, but rather over in the West Wing. And the Oval Office was decorated in white whereas this room was all decorated in blue. Then she remembered a broadcast on shelters for the needy that the President had given three months earlier. It had been from this room, the Blue Room. That was it. While the room was gorgeous, it was the tree that dominated.

"It must be six meters tall."

"Eighteen feet this year. They delivered it by a horse-drawn wagon, can you believe that in this day and age? And, no, the decorations this year are not on your behalf. I didn't even think about that until today."

Genny focused on the ornaments, through the dazzle of the beautiful lighting. The lights themselves were flags, national flags. Made of Tiffany glass.

"The flags of the U.N.?" This was becoming a little creepy. Genny almost felt as if the President were stalking her.

"No. The League of Nations. I have been doing so much work with the U.N. this last year that it seemed appropriate to honor the first attempt to form a world government for peace. And it humbles me to remember that this nation, that worked so hard to create the League, was even then too divided to join it."

"Do you remember the name of the room where we first met?"

"Not really. Wait, maybe I do. The Woodrow Wilson Reading Room."

"Which is filled with the card catalog for the League of Nations."

"Really? I guess this looks pretty bad?"

"It doesn't look good, Mr. President."

He turned back to inspect the tree. "I just meant it to honor the League."

Genny studied the profile of the man studying the tree. Here stood a thoughtful man, but perhaps also a humble one. He had little of the arrogance she expected from the senior official of the United States of America. He had used his own tree to remind himself that he could do better if he just kept trying. How rare such men were.

She could feel this moment, this place somehow shifting around her. Genny always felt her way up to decision points, had learned to trust her instincts.

Many of her instincts said that the proper action was to remove her grip from his elbow and ask the nice Secret Service lady to get her out of this room, this building, and off these premises. Quickly.

There was no way in which she could keep her life, which she loved, and yet even consider staying in the room with this man due to the merest possibility of where it might lead.

And then the oddest thing happened.

Rather than letting go and allowing her to run, her gloved hand squeezed his arm. She leaned in and whispered, against all better judgment, "It is a beautiful tree."

She assessed her reaction for having acted so irrationally. And was intrigued to discover that it settled as lightly as the tiny spaceships, disguised as snow, fluttering down outside the bay window of the White House.

Chapter 2

The President's idea of a "small reception" in the Residence was much in keeping with Genny's idea of what it turned out to be. She had been to enough political receptions throughout her career not to be surprised by this one.

Thirty or so guests, a half dozen waiters, and a trio of Secret Service agents milled about the Central Hall of the second floor of the Residence. Actually the Secret Service didn't so much mill about as stand unobtrusively, looking like black-suited structural pillars in a room otherwise done in white, pale yellow, and abounding with Christmas décor.

Small trees, not much taller than she was, were placed in three corners of the spacious room. A grand piano and harp stood in the fourth corner. The instruments did not intrude even halfway into the width of the space and had no impact at all upon its length. The musicians played Christmas carols, but softly enough that conversation was possible without raising your voice. Evergreen garlands draped above portraits of past Presidents and scenes of rural America.

Tables laden with canapés, crudités, spiced nuts, and other hors d'oeuvres were scattered down the length of the hall. Each table sported a centerpiece of a Christmas scene done in elegant gingerbread complete with lights and sugared walkways. She was absolutely and completely charmed.

Genny was also pleased to see that she had judged the attire appropriately. The President had said casual, and the White House Social Secretary had been able to translate that for her as, "The men will all be in suits. Though several will shed their ties after they get clear of the news cameras, the President will not. The women will not be in evening gowns, but most will wear designer slacks, tailored blouse, and a warm but attractive jacket fr protection against the cold." She'd opted for Weizmann boots, Dior pants, a dark silk blouse, and a silver satin Asian jacket with black dragon brocade. Her only jewelry, a thin silver chain about her neck bearing a small pendant of the Chinese ideogram for "Serenity" that no one had yet recognized nor asked the meaning.

She was chatting pleasantly enough with the Chairman of the Joint Chiefs of Staff. He might be the highest ranking officer in the U.S. military, but General Brett Rogers had also been an Army Private forty years earlier, while serving at the end of the Vietnam War.

"By the time I arrived, Saigon was about as far north as a grunt could go. I was there less than a year before it was all over, spent most of it out on the Mekong Delta."

"I imagine that was not the most pleasant of assignments." Genny was reminding herself to be civil. This man had been fighting in the Vietnamese swamps, while her family had retreated to the safety of their ancestral village in the Languedoc region of southern France. They had escaped in the early 1960s and had not returned to Vietnam until the mid-1970s after the war was over.

"It wasn't," General Rogers agreed. "But I did love the countryside. I come from Fargo, North Dakota, one of our Great Plains states, and had never seen anything else like it. Amazing places and people, at least the ones not trying to kill a nineteen-year-old punk kid who wet his pants in his first battle."

People in the Matthews' White House kept not being what she expected. She'd expected a grizzled warrior who despised her country, yet he didn't. And the highest-rank soldier in their country had just confessed to being afraid.

"Are you monopolizing the second prettiest woman in the room, Brett?" Daniel Drake Darlington, the White House Chief of Staff, joined them. Speaking of beautiful men, he was quite the most beautiful one in the room. He looked like the magazine ad for blond surfers rather than the most powerful non-elected person in the country. Her little sister would go crazy if she ever met him, he was exactly her type.

"Second?" Genny hadn't meant it to sound borderline petty. There were a number of astonishingly well-maintained women here.

"Well, my apologies, but I do have a bias for my wife. Alice is here somewhere."

Brett harrumphed, "Damn woman knows more about my troop movements than I do."

"She's an analyst for the CIA," Daniel explained to Genny, a point that clearly gave him great pride.

"Good one too," the General agreed. Then he spotted someone over Genny's shoulder. "Oh no! Well, there goes the neighborhood." But the General's smile, the first she'd seen on his face, appeared quite genuine. "Emily, over here."

She turned in time to see a stunning blond walking beside President Matthews. They were similar in height. The woman's posture was impeccable, her walk so perfectly balanced that Genny knew she was exceptionally trained even without the green dress-uniform she wore. And she and the President moved with an easy familiarity that went far beyond mere friendship.

If he had a woman like this at his side, what in all the world was she doing here? Was that a stab of jealousy she felt? It was like meeting Lauren Bacall, who she had, or Meryl Streep, who she hadn't, and finding them on the arm of the man she had thought… Where those thoughts had arisen, she didn't know. Genny focused on kicking them back beneath the metaphoric jungle foliage of her mind. Even as she did so, she knew one thing for certain, she'd just been totally outclassed.

The President had invited her to Washington, D.C. for a tree-lighting ceremony and a drink. No more. *Remets-t'en!* She had surely been put in her place. She waited a heartbeat or two and checked in with herself. Nope, she wasn't over it yet.

The woman saluted the General.

"None of that here," Brett Rogers grumbled, but returned the salute so sharply that there was no mistaking how much he liked the woman.

"Major Emily Beale, Geneviève Beauchamp of UNESCO." The President introduced them. "Emily is presently on leave. She's the best friend from my childhood and perhaps of my present. And…" He turned to apply an introductory label to Genny and found—nothing.

Genny refused to be embarrassed, but found that choice very difficult to uphold. The swirl of her constantly shifting emotions over the last hour was making her head hurt.

Emily watched the President for a merciless second before extending her hand. "Well, you have totally flustered him, which is actually hard to do. He must be very attracted to you. Therefore, you and I had better start right off with first names. Call me Emily."

"Genny." The woman's handshake was warm and genuine and went a long way to easing Genny's nerves.

"Genny?" the President protested. "You're making me call you Geneviève."

"And that requirement, it remains not changed."

Emily laughed while the President sputtered. "I like you, Genny Beauchamp. I think we're going to become good friends. Keep him on his toes, it's good for him."

Genny nodded her agreement uncertainly. Emily was close to the President, but perhaps not with him? She needed a guidebook.

"Where did a UNESCO senior manager acquire those calluses?"

"How do you know I am a senior manager?" Genny clenched her hands, feeling the comfort of the hard-won calluses. Had this woman, this friend of the President been briefed on Genny's background along with who knew how many others?

"The way you carry yourself. Poise and calm in this setting," Emily's circling finger indicated the present company of the President, his Chief of Staff, and the Chairman of the Joint Chiefs. Then a nod toward the dozen or more Washington elite scattered about the room.

Genny nodded, feeling only a little foolish. It made sense. Emily Beale was simply a trained, perceptive woman. So, seeing no reason to evade, Genny held out her hand and turned it palm up. The President leaned forward in surprise to inspect it.

"Vovinam Việt Võ Đạo," Genny pointed to the primary calluses that Emily had noticed in a simple handshake. "Vietnamese martial arts. Those calluses are mostly from staff. I like staff."

"What degree?"

"Yellow, third Dan."

Emily faced Peter and then laughed right in the President's face. It seemed disrespectful, but his friend was clearly enjoying the President's perplexity. She took his shoulder and shook him easily. None of the Secret Service reacted, so this wasn't anything unusual between them. A part of Genny still wondered what was usual.

"What's so funny?" A big, broad-shouldered man arrived beside Emily Beale and slipped a hand around her waist. He also wore Dress Greens, saluted the General in a friendly fashion far less formal than Emily's had been, then clapped the White House Chief of Staff solidly on the shoulder in greeting. His eyes were as strikingly gray as Emily's were blue.

Emily kissed him on the cheek, which made Genny feel actively stupid for thinking there had been something between her and the President beyond friendship. Emily was exactly as the President had introduced her. An old friend.

"Peter has found a very pleasant UNESCO official who is a Việt Võ Đạo third Dan."

The newcomer laughed as well, then turned to inspect her. His eyes did a quick flicker down her length, but she didn't feel offended. It wasn't as if he were a male admiring her attributes. Instead, she felt as if she'd just been very carefully assessed for weapons and any other potential surprises.

"Mr. President," he had a deep voice obviously used to command. He also clearly didn't share Emily's "Peter" privileges with his Commander-in-Chief, or perhaps he did, but chose not to exercise them.

"Third Dan means she's a third-level Instructor just an edge below being a Master. Can see it in her posture and balance." He stuck out a large hand which she shook gladly. "Major Mark Henderson at your service. Do you find much occasion for using your martial arts in the Council Chamber at the U.N.?"

"My specialty is World Heritage Sites in Southeast Asia. I frequently must work with tribal leaders, military factions, warlords, and the like. I have not yet had to use those skills, Major Henderson, but I do appreciate having them."

"Perhaps you haven't needed to use them because they can see you already have them. Do you play poker?"

"No poker. But my two sisters and I play a mean Scrabble game though."

"You do?" The President brightened significantly while the other four in the circle groaned. "Ignore these heathens. Let me go find a board."

He turned as if to start the search immediately, but Emily hooked a wrist and with a simple twist, that Genny knew would cause sharp pain if ignored, brought the President back to the circle.

Genny wasn't sure, but she thought she caught the flicker of a smile on the big Secret Service agent standing at the wall.

"You have a room full of guests, Peter. You two can play games later." Emily's smile showed that she knew perfectly well the double-entendre she'd just offered.

Genny inspected the circle of friends that surrounded the President. For there was no question that while these people served at the pleasure of the President, they also truly enjoyed his company. It was a high recommendation of the man indeed.

For the second time that night, Genny did something that felt right though it ran counter to her better judgment. She tucked a hand around his elbow, no glove and heavy wool coat to separate them this time. His light jacket and linen shirt was all that kept them from touching. She could feel the difference in closeness.

"Do not worry, Mr. President Matthews." She made her voice as sexy as possible, playing up her French accent, knowing its affect on Americans. "We can play games in, perhaps, a later time."

He blushed bright red and the rest of them laughed.

Only Genny felt the slight pressure on her fingers as he squeezed her hand with a bend of his elbow. It was a very welcoming gesture.

# # #

Peter was wholly bemused.

It was past midnight. He'd shed his jacket and his tie and sat in the middle of the Central Hall on a low sofa.

Across the coffee table, Geneviève Beauchamp was the only remaining guest. Frank and Beatrice had retired to the far end of the Hall to guard unobtrusively while the woman massacred him on the Scrabble board. Maybe he should retreat back to playing on-line, at there he pretty much dominated. Too bad he couldn't play in the National Championships without actually attending.

Her silvered jacket was unbuttoned, but still draped upon her shoulders. Her hair, pulled forward over one shoulder, flowed in a lush dark wave. She leaned forward to study the Scrabble board, so that a small Chinese medallion she wore spun and sparkled with each movement. She was absolutely breathtaking.

"Enfilade, Mr. President." She'd spent six out of seven letters in her tray around the "AD" already on the board. The four-point "F," he was chagrined to notice, had landed on a triple-letter score. They had sat down hours before to play a single game to two hundred points. He'd foolishly given her the first move and she'd emptied her entire tray on the first play with "Debacle" gaining a quick eighty points including the bonus for playing all seven letters. They hadn't stopped at two-hundred points, they'd stopped when the tiles ran out.

Now they were on their third game and she was close to her second win. He thanked god that her final letter hadn't been playable or the point bonus for emptying her entire tray yet again would have locked up the game.

Frank, the head of his Presidential Protection Detail, would play with him when Peter was at loose ends, but they rarely finished those games. Peter did some of his best thinking while playing Scrabble with Frank as it left his subconscious free to nibble away at a political problem. The head of his PPD didn't appear to mind losing, or mind having the game interrupted once Peter had solved the problem.

With Geneviève, he had to completely concentrate and still it was a hard fight.

"Enfilade. Most appropriate, as you have just shot up my two best plays. And you still aren't calling me Peter."

"You are correct again, Mr. President." She drew four letters then shook the bag. Empty. The end was imminent and he needed a brilliant play to salvage his position.

"Why is that? And why am I calling you Geneviève, despite the 'Genny' liberties you offer to everyone else?"

"First, Mr. President, you are a head of state, I am not."

He grinned. Sparring with her was so much fun. "And second?"

"Your play."

"And second?" He sat back on the couch and crossed his arms over his chest making it clear that he wasn't going to play until she answered.

Now she looked up at him from her intent study of the board. He had expected her look of deep concentration, or perhaps the funny tease that had made him so enjoy her company, but instead it was a soft and somewhat bewildered expression that she presented.

"Perhaps it would be best if I go."

Peter came to his feet and extended a hand to help her to her feet. A lady said it was time to go, then it was time. No questions asked. At least not on that front.

"And second?"

But she didn't answer him. They walked side by side down the Grand Staircase, sweeping the two Secret Service agents before them. At the North Portico entrance, there was already a car waiting. Wishing he'd thought to put his jacket back on before stepping out into the freezing air, they stopped together for a moment on the outside steps.

"No clichés now," he warned her.

"I was not planning on one, Mr. President." Then she took both of his hands in hers.

He still couldn't feel the calluses, though he could feel the startling strength in those fine fingers.

"And second," she acknowledged his earlier question. "I will ask that you continue to call me Geneviève. For I do so enjoy how it sounds when you say it." She lifted up lightly on her toes and offered him a kiss on each cheek in the French style, and then a chaste, but not overly hasty one on his lips.

He held the car door for her as she climbed in. Then she spoke once more just before he could close it.

"If you play 'Redacted' on the 'E' I left open in 'Enfilade,' it will be your game, Mr. President."

Then she was gone, and he was left rocking on his heels. She'd counted each of the tiled letters that had been played, knowing that the bag was empty and what she had on her own tray.

"Wave, Mr. President," Frank Adams, the head of his protection detail, whispered at him softly.

So he did.

"She's got you, Sir."

He watched the taillights as Agent Belfour drove Geneviève Beauchamp off the White House grounds.

"Got you real bad," Frank was practically chortling.

There was certainly no chance of him redacting that bit of truth before everyone around him knew it.

Chapter 3

Genny received a nasty surprise over her room-service breakfast, but it took her a while before she found out about it. The White House had reserved Genny a room at The Hay-Adams Hotel. She'd had to close the curtains quickly on entering the room, for it had offered a clear view of the White House Residence directly across Lafayette Square Park and that had been just too much to think about.

She'd held herself together for the short ride to the Hay. It probably would have been faster to walk the two blocks, but her knees weren't really up to it, so she was quite appreciative of Agent Belfour's escort.

Once she was alone, then the nerves set in. President Peter Matthews, the leader of the American people, consumed her thoughts. Throughout the evening he had been charming, thoughtful, funny, and most importantly, real. Throughout the reception and then the Scrabble game he had simply been himself; laughing, casual, self-deprecating. He had granted her a thoroughly enjoyable evening. She knew better than to trust it. Gérard and she had any number of wonderful evenings, right until they'd become married.

Genny had married straight out of Cambridge University. Gérard had been beautiful, wealthy, and wholly incompatible. In so many ways: political views, disposition, temper. His desire to travel beyond Europe had been non-existent and she had missed home too much.

The lush warmth and easy friendships of Vietnam had beckoned her too strongly. She and Gérard hadn't lasted six months.

In the years since, her career had broken even more relationships than it had made. She had climbed quickly at UNESCO. Her ability to obtain needed permissions from governments and locals alike to preserve culturally important sites had quickly catapulted her up the ladder. She was the Head of Section for Southeast Asia, which meant that she was more frequently in Paris at the World Heritage Center than in her own homeland.

And now, she was finding that shifting her attention to New York had allowed her unprecedented access to U.N. Ambassadors and hence the ear of their countries' leaderships.

Her work had led her to live much of the year in America, but her life was not here. It no longer resided in any one place. It was scattered across the globe. She rarely came to rest, but that was a lifestyle that worked for her. Genny could imagine no other way of being.

Yet, sitting last night with the President, just the two of them, had been comfortable. Despite the surreal setting and the unexpected company, she had felt oddly relaxed. As if it were a perfectly normal evening to be sitting in the Central Hall with the President and enjoying a game and friendly conversation as the house quieted. As the White House quieted. And that thought had only wound her nerves back up once more.

But Peter, it was comfortable to think of him that way, though surprisingly difficult to speak so, hadn't offered up some heirloom, valuable first edition, or ornate Scrabble board. Instead, it was old and worn—maroon cardboard, a cracking seam down the center, and well-worn letters in a brown paper lunch sack. And a heavily thumbed dictionary. An American one, so all of the handy Scottish words that had a "Q" without a "U" hadn't been allowed.

It was when she ordered room service that she received her nasty surprise. Along with a Lemon Ricotta Pancake with berries and American maple syrup, one of America's great contributions to international cuisine, came the morning's *Washington Post*.

The front page of Post had a grainy photo, obviously taken with a long telephoto lens at night. It was her chaste kiss with the President last night. But it didn't look chaste. "Mystery Woman Necking President" was the headline over the photo. Obviously late to press, it referred to page A14 for the rest of the story.

Page A14 had another photo of them walking arm in arm away from the Christmas Tree, identifiable only because of her long hair and his bodyguards. That was all they had, not even her name. But last night's guest list would provide that soon enough.

Her first instinct was to call the President and apologize.

Her second instinct was to scream in rage. It had been so pleasant and now it was tainted, made lurid by the American so-called journalists.

Thankfully, rational thought quashed that so quickly that it barely had an opportunity to raise its ugly head. The Americans were so very uptight about such matters. It didn't really effect her after all. Let them have their games.

Then her phone rang and her forkful of pancake flipped from her fingers and fell to the carpet. She swept it up quickly hoping that it didn't leave much of a stain on the immaculate white surface. What sort of a crazy hotel used white carpet?

With three phones in the room, she only had to reach for the one at her window-side dining table. When she answered, perhaps a little tentatively, she was asked to please hold for the President.

"I'm so sorry about this," Peter launched right in when he came on the line. His complete lack of morning niceties was so American that it made her smile. "I suppose we should have been somewhat more discrete."

"Mr. President, it is not my problem, but rather it is yours."

"Ah," he paused for a long moment. She could almost see him looking for a piece of paper or a pen to fool around with while he considered his response. "Clearly you've only seen the paper this morning, and not the television news."

"Ah, yourself." She fought against the irritation she felt as she understood what he was saying. "So, if it is now my problem, that would imply that your American media must be already camped in front of my hotel. They probably also watch the rear exits. I have heard of such foolishness. You really must fix those laws. Your so-cherished American Freedom of the Press has been taken past reason. What of Right to Privacy, I ask you?" The photo in the paper glared, garish in poor color. She flipped it face down.

"The Fourth Amendment promises security against unreasonable search and seizure. It states nothing regarding privacy."

"Therefore I am thinking that your country does not think. In my home country, we have far fewer laws and far more respect."

"We think very hard. However, that does not imply that what we have evolved over time necessarily makes any sense."

Genny considered what it must mean to be President of such a place. And how much she was enjoying this discussion, despite the topic. She had slept little last night for several reasons, but the main one had been that she'd felt vitalized by his attention. As if he brought some part of her to life with which she was unfamiliar.

"If you are thinking so hard, Mr. President, what are you thinking?"

"I'm thinking," his voice was suddenly warmer and softer, as if he were whispering into the phone. "That I don't care about any picture as long as I get the chance to kiss you again."

She laughed. Genny couldn't help herself. It was like a release of something deep inside. A part of her that a succession of arrogant men had frozen, she'd feared permanently.

"I think, Mr. President, that will cause no end of trouble for both of us, but," she had to be honest, "it is something I too should like to try."

"Excellent! So when can I see you again?"

"I was planning to return to New York this evening after my annual visit to the museum."

"Which museum?"

"Air and Space."

Again his laugh was warm in her ear, "Not Art, or Natural History?"

"Smithsonian Air and Space, the Udvar-Hazy Center, in Virginia." She had to raise her voice over his laughter. "What do you find so amusing about me, Mr. President?"

"About you? That's perfect. That is what I find so amusing. That you are never what I expect."

Genny had no good answer to that and fooled around with the cooling pancake on her plate. Her ex-husband, past lovers, and even casual dates had always formed a neatly structured *casier* in their minds for her to belong inside of. It had made her very angry. This man, the first in her experience, was filled with joy so that it burst out of him, precisely because she didn't fit into a neat pigeon's hole.

"Hold on a minute, if you would."

He was back in under thirty seconds.

"It seems that my evening is free. Perhaps we could meet at the museum at six o'clock. I'm booked solid starting five minutes ago, but Daniel can handle the two meetings after six."

"It closes at five-thirty, Mr. President."

"Yes, it does."

Genny's position had more than once afforded her entry into a cultural site when it was technically closed. On such visits there was a sense of peace and you could feel the air prickling with anticipation and possibility, just as they must have felt when they were first formed. Yet she had never entered a major museum after hours. She could catch an early train tomorrow and still be in time for her first meeting.

"That is something I will be looking forward to, Mr. President."

# # #

"You never said why this particular museum, Geneviève." Peter looked about the massive hangar of the Smithsonian National Air and Space Museum's Udvar-Hazy Center at the south end of Dulles International Airport. He'd never actually been to this one, or known it was so close. Just twenty minutes outside of D.C., the two massive hangars had hundreds of aircraft. It was a kaleidoscopic whirl, so many wings, fuselages, and markings that his eyes had trouble separating one from the next.

The first hangar had been dominated by four massive planes: the Enola Gay that dropped the Hiroshima bomb and the Boeing Dash-80 that proved the viability of passenger jets. Close beside her was her extreme offspring, the Concorde and at the far end of the hangar stood an SR-71 Blackbird Mach 3 spy plane that could fly twenty miles high.

In one corner of the hangar, Geneviève led him on a tour of the various aircraft that had shaped Vietnam's history. The MiG-15 and the F-14 Tomcat jet fighters loomed above them, but it was the helicopters that had intrigued him. He knew that Emily had started out in a Huey UH-1 Iroquois.

"We captured one of these on our plantation. Gram used it for transporting a new roasting oven for the coffee before turning it over to the government. Then she let the pilot loose in the woods with a map and a compass, it was the best she could do for him. She received a thank you letter many years later from Alabama."

Peter had flown in both the White Hawk and bigger Sea King versions of Marine One and Emily's Black Hawk. Modern thoroughbreds compared to the Huey and the even more ungainly Seahorse parked close beside it. These machines were primitive by comparison.

Geneviève had let him look his fill, and now they were headed into the other hangar. A museum manager had made himself discretely available, though it hadn't taken him long to fade back in with the Secret Service agents. He and Frank appeared to hit it off well, and he clearly liked Beat, which left Peter feeling as if he had Geneviève to himself.

Their footsteps echoed as they turned between a Messerschmitt and the American version of Hitler's V-1 Buzz Bomb. The whole museum was so quiet, he could practically hear the planes sleeping.

"This passage always gives me hope, Mr. President. So much of the Boeing Aviation Hangar is filled with machines of war. This hangar is much different."

They stepped through the brightly lit tunnel into the vast dimness of the next hangar. The vista slowly opened before them. At first he couldn't make sense of the black, bulbous nose that confronted him. A little farther down, the tunnel the vista opened before him and he stumbled to a halt. He'd known it was here somewhere, but that hadn't prepared him for the impact.

The space shuttle *Discovery* dominated the space before him. It looked as if it had just now landed, surprisingly world-worn. All of the other craft had been so clean that they might have been manufactured just for the museum. Not the shuttle. Its tiles were discolored. It showed the wear and tear of dozens of missions, scorch marks on her white paint, yet still she stood proudly.

"This especially I wanted to see, Mr. President."

"Why is that?"

She clucked her tongue at him causing him to focus on her. "Clearly you forget my history."

"Your history? Now you're going to give me more lessons," he complained. He made it funny, fully acknowledging that the President of the United States was indeed whining. The amount she knew about this museum had staggered him.

"Yes, Mr. President your history is lacking and you need a lesson."

He tried a sulking pout and she laughed.

"That makes you look like angry two-year old."

"So, give me your lesson, Section Chief Beauchamp," he pouted harder.

She managed to keep a straight face, but it was clearly a struggle. She finally had to turn away and release a set of girlish giggles that echoed back to them off the high, curved metal ceiling. Catching her breath, she turned back to him.

"A very good friend of my grandfather flew on a Soyuz in 1980, they were in the VPAF together. What you would call the North Vietnamese Air Force, they both flew in that MiG-15 we just saw. He was made a Hero of the Soviet Union for shooting down one of your B-52 bombers, though your country continues to deny the incident a half century later. I also have an uncle, from the French side of the family, who flew on your space shuttle in 1992. Flew for the 'other side' if you will. Just because we are Vietnamese does not mean that we are not modern."

"Well," he gazed at her for a moment. "We Americans are innately arrogant."

"I was thinking it is acquired later in life."

"No, it's genetic. We're born that way. So, is this the shuttle he flew on?"

"The *Columbia*. But now she too is a casualty of war, though the battle was with space."

Thoughts of that shuttle disintegrating during reentry and killing the crew sobered them. They circled the craft in silence, gazing at the exhibits off to either side, but ultimately returning to the *Discovery*. When they had fully circled the craft, Peter noticed a long ladder leading up to a small circular hatch in the side. It was open and the light from within shone out into the hangar like a beacon in the night.

Geneviève looked longingly at the ladder, and Peter had to admit that… He waved over the hangar manager.

"Mr. Emerson, I don't suppose that we could," he pointed up the ladder, feeling stupid for even asking. It was clearly not designed for public usage.

"The exhibit curator suggested that you might wish to look inside. I admit, I took the opportunity to sit aboard her myself before she went on display. It was quite the experience."

# # #

Genny was in shock that she was climbing the ladder into the actual space shuttle. She'd never dreamed that she'd get to do such a thing. Ducking in through the small lock, she stood, and was immediately disappointed.

A couple of blue chairs with massive seatbelts filled much of the small space, little bigger than the bedroom of her Paris apartment; which was not saying much, especially at Parisian prices. No windows, no views. The walls were all covered in near-identical cabinet drawers. Most bore some incomprehensible label, equipment to fix things. She understood a few: tile repair kit, avionics spares, food stuffs. She tried to pull open that one, but it wouldn't move. The curator, who had come in behind her and Peter, showed them how to release the catch to either side. Of course it couldn't just pull open, not in space. Sadly, the drawer was empty.

A small corridor led forward, but a quick peek revealed more cabinets and storage lockers. Aft was a big round hatch, that must lead out to the Payload Bay beneath the giant doors on the back of the ship.

"It is all so tiny."

"Normally three to five crew members are in this space, along with their space suits," the curator pointed out. "They did not send much empty space into space." It was clearly one of his pat lines, so she laughed dutifully.

Then he indicated for her to climb the ladder that she'd missed on her first scan of the room. It climbed upward steeply.

"The proportions are all wrong," Peter observed. And he was right.

Her hands, holding onto the two verticals, were too far apart and the steps impossibly steep.

"Spacesuits and weightlessness," she and the curator said in near unison.

Then she finished the climb to the Flight Deck. This was spectacular. Smaller than the area below, it felt huge. Peter actually had to nudge her aside as she gawked. Banks of switches and controls covered almost every surface. There were three seats. One faced rearward, placed before the controls and window that looked out into the Payload Bay. The other two seats faced forward, looking out over the entrance from the Boeing Hanger. She glanced for permission, then slipped into the left hand seat. Peter into the right.

A large joystick fit her hand, though clearly it could also be used while wearing a spacesuit's heavy gloves.

"You, Ms. Beauchamp," the curator was still being obsequiously polite in the President's presence, "have chosen the Shuttle Commander's seat. That makes the President your pilot."

"Good, that is where you should be, Mr. President. At the command of the woman." Out of the corner of her eye, she could see him smiling at her in a strange way. So she carefully didn't look over, but instead inspected the controls before them. A half dozen screens, as big as the ones on her laptop, were arranged in front of her. From them, in every direction, ranged banks of switches, readouts, and rotary knobs. Some in bright red with special covers. One even needed a key, marked incomprehensibly as "RJDA 18." She pointed it out to Peter.

"So, is that the one to make your seat like an ejector seat? What if we get into space and I forget to bring the key?"

"Did you always want to go to space, Commander Beauchamp?"

"No, I would have liked to fly, but I fell in love with the ancient temples and beautiful scenery. Did you always want to be President, Mr. Pilot?"

At his silence, Genny looked over at him. That's when she also noticed that the curator had tactfully withdrawn, leaving them to their momentary dreams of space.

Peter smiled slowly, but looked forward out the windows. She wondered what he saw other than the high ceilings of the hangar in which they sat.

"No. What I always wanted to do was help people to reach a better understanding. Never thought about politics until my wife came up with it." He said "wife" as if even that brief mention hurt him, and she was sorry she had caused such a bad memory to return. "Becoming President was simply a way to do that on a scale I hadn't previously imagined."

Genny needed a subject change, as that had all become much too solemn.

"Weren't you like other little boys, Mr. President? Didn't you want to go flying into space?"

"No. Flying was Em's dream, not mine." His smile became soft and wistful.

"How is it that you did not end up married to Emily?" Genny still couldn't make sense of that, they appeared so close. Even closer, or at least more familiar, than she was with her husband.

Peter turned to face her now, turning away from whatever visions lay beyond the shuttle's windows. His unblinking gaze riveted her to her chair. She couldn't look away if the shuttle were crashing and it was up to her to save it.

"I thought that at one time. But Emily was smarter than I was and ran, and I mean that literally, ran in the other direction." Then he turned back to the window and gazed out into the lights.

Genny left him to his thoughts for a long time.

Then he blinked as if coming abruptly back to the present. His smile wiped away any of the gloom that had hovered over his features.

"Besides, the one time I kissed her, it was like kissing my sister, if I had one. It just didn't work at all."

Chapter 4

G*enny leaned back in* the luxury of The Beast. The Presidential Limousine might be a heavily armored rolling fortress, but it was also very, very comfortable. The leather bucket seat wrapped around her. Though if not for the wide, shared armrest, she'd be rubbing shoulders with the President.

"I thought your car would be wider. It feels very narrow."

The President rapped his knuckles on the side panel of the car door as they zipped from the museum back to the White House with a full police escort. "Five inches of bullet-proof protection on all sides has to go somewhere."

They turned in at the gates to the White House.

"I am not returning to my hotel?"

"I was hoping that you would join me for a late dinner. You don't mind, do you?"

Genny began considering the various implications and then stopped. She didn't want their evening to be over, and that was enough for her. At least for now.

"My family may still be too French, we rarely dine before this time. Can you cook?"

"Not even a little bit. I can barbeque, but not cook. You?"

"I do not even do that." Genny had always loved food, just not enough to learn to prepare it for herself. And living so much on the road made any effort to maintain a kitchen utterly pointless. She didn't even have a place to stay other than her family's house on the plantation and her own a small apartment in Paris close by the World Heritage offices. Everything else was hotel rooms.

She noted that they pulled up to the South Portico, rather than the North. And that a canopy like a hotel's shielded the path from the car door to the White House doors.

"You are afraid to be photographed with me?" The journey to the museum had included an elaborate shell game in which Agent Belfour had led her through the Hay-Adams basement to the church on the other side of the street, and she had been driven separately from the President.

"No," Peter hesitated, then confirmed his initial response as if making it more true for himself. "No. I don't mind. I had thought to shield you from too much media attention for your own sake."

Usually Genny found men to be so easy to read, but with the President she had such difficulty that it was hard to be sure. Was he making it up on her behalf or did he not want the negative press? Like that movie, this President had absurdly high approval from the American people. But unlike the movie, he was not facing an election for two more years. Could he afford a girlfriend? Was that something she wanted to be? Too many questions.

"How is it that you know so little about me? Didn't your Secret Service investigate me? Even more now that I am seeing you a second time?" She remained seated in the car, so he made no move to open the door. She could just see his bodyguard waiting beside the car door, partially hidden by the thick glass as well as by the shadows beneath the canopy.

"I'm sure they did." The President turned on the light inside the passenger compartment.

Now she could see him more clearly, but she understood him no better.

"I asked for information about you after our first meeting in July," he continued. "They told me three things about you: your name, your job title, and that you had avoided any chance at having a decent education by attending Cambridge. I have asked them to tell me nothing else about you."

"You must have attended that second-rate place in the Midlands."

They shared a smile over the centuries-old rivalry between their schools of Cambridge and Oxford.

"They told you nothing?" Genny had assumed that she was operating at an immense disadvantage in this relationship. That her life was an open book to a man who she only knew through his public image.

"Nothing. I ordered them not to."

She'd have to think about that.

Assuming he was telling the truth, it meant that he was being decent and fair far past any man she had ever met. And she could think of no reason for him to lie.

"So you asked me to come to the White House because I caught your eye?" If he said yes, he might become the third man she tried her martial arts on.

"While you are shockingly beautiful, no."

Even if she didn't tie her ego to her looks, the compliment washed over her and added to the warmth she was beginning to feel for the man. A warmth that was spreading far past her thoughts.

"It was that you, as a woman, talked three Southeast Asian U.N. Ambassadors to a standstill without even breaking a sweat."

"Breaking a sweat?" She knew a great deal of American idiom, but not that piece.

"You made it look effortless."

"Ah."

"And I thought that this was a woman worth knowing. I see your beauty as a mere bonus." His smile turned slightly wicked.

"And now you are baiting me. Well, I shall rise above it and you will now take me to dinner in your house."

The President knocked twice on the window with the back of his knuckles. After he helped her out of the car, he did not release her hand while escorting her inside.

# # #

They sat together in the Second Floor Kitchen. The staff had tried to place them in the formal dining room, but Geneviève had asked if they could simply dine at the island in the kitchen.

Peter had liked the sound of that.

Once dinner had been delivered from the main kitchen in the basement, he'd dismissed both the staff and the Secret Service. He knew the latter had merely retired to wait on the floor below until relieved by the next shift or Geneviève was ready to go home. Which he hoped wasn't anytime soon. Not only was he enjoying her company, but she was also a joy to watch. Not merely the sleek red dress with ornate golden needlework that wrapped so splendidly about her body.

When she spoke, her hands came to life. She would fold them quietly when being an attentive listener, and then, as she attempted to draw some mental image, her hands rose and sculpted the air about her until it vibrated with her energy. It was as if she pulled threads of Peter himself and made them glow in the air before her.

He kept wishing he had looked at her Secret Service file, then he might not feel as if he was constantly in over his head. But that boat had long since sailed. She simply overwhelmed him every moment they were together. Like now, they didn't even need to be speaking. They simply sat quietly and enjoyed their dessert of coconut ice cream with dark chocolate sauce.

They sat on barstools across the maple-wood island from each other in his private kitchen, a room he rarely used for more than a late-night scrambled eggs and toast. It was unfamiliar in many ways, but she made him feel as if he had sat here many times. With her. It was as if the room had been waiting only for her to place the final, proper accent upon it. She brought it too to life. The walnut cabinets picked up the highlights in her dark hair. Her eyes shone brighter than the brass fittings in the soft glow of the candles he had discovered in a corner cabinet.

He did his best not to compare her to his first wife, but it was inevitable. Katherine Matthews had been the center of attention in any room she entered. A red-headed whirlwind with a siren's body who had bowled him off his feet before he knew what hit him. Yet by the time they arrived at the White House they were barely on speaking terms.

She had lived on the third floor of the Residence, he'd lived on the second. To this day, he couldn't stand to go up there. Being a lone bachelor in the entire Residence had felt too foolish. When he made Daniel his Chief of Staff, he'd also given him the third floor to live in. Now he and his wife Alice resided there, and best of luck to them. It made the perfect excuse for him not to go up there. When the three of them dined together, which was several times a week when their schedule at the White House or Alice's at the CIA didn't interfere, they met on the second floor or over in the West Wing dining room.

Katherine had staked out her territory with her vivacity, her immense popularity, her slap-you-in-the-face sexual power, and a conniving streak a mile wide that had been her ultimate undoing.

Geneviève carried an air of quiet sophistication about her. Her temper was as placid as a mountain lake. Granted, one of unknown depths, but she was a center of calm. He felt better just for sitting with her. Even the first time Peter had met Katherine, she'd left him feeling drained.

He had to give his dead wife some credit, he wouldn't be President without her. She'd pushed and driven, arranged and maneuvered until he'd met all of the right people and been in all of the right places. Her sense of politics had far exceeded his own. In that one way, they had been a good team. She navigated the political landscape as if she had her own personal, private, executive roadmap.

His interests had lain elsewhere. What drove him to the Presidency was the opportunity to make a difference. He'd been a key player in dozens of corporate rescues, eventually including the restructuring of NASA and recovering whole sections of the auto industry that had teetered on the brink of bankruptcy. It's where he'd made his name and where he'd found his joy.

And it had nothing to do with Katherine. That part of his life, at least, was clean from the blemishes she had laid upon so much of his life.

But he didn't want to think about her. He wanted to know more about the passions of the woman sharing his dinner table.

"Tell me more about your Heritage Sites, Geneviève."

# # #

Over the long-finished meal, a very passable Thai curry on red rice and magnificent coconut ice cream, Genny told the President of a few of the dozens of wonders she'd toured, both in Southeast Asia and other places around the world. From the Phong Nha-Ke Bang Park of Vietnam, the largest karst limestone cave system on the planet, where the largest cave in the world had only been discovered in 2009, large enough to hold a New York City block, including its forty-story high skyscrapers. To the Buddhist Temple of Borobudur in Indonesia, lost for six hundred years in the jungle and second only to Angkor Wat. She'd also entered the Caves of Lascaux, not the replica that had been set up for tourists, but the original, now so carefully protected against further degradation due to moisture.

"I had to wear a rebreathing apparatus simply to keep the moisture from my breath from touching the paintings."

"And I'll bet you looked fetching in it."

Genny was beginning to trust her perception of the President's thoughts. By his smile, he clearly was thinking of how she must have looked in some sexy James Bond movie heroine fashion. It was hard to complain that he saw her in such a way. Though eventually reality would disappoint. But in the favor of his more practical side, his constant questions and interruptions proved he was also paying attention to her words.

Not only did he appear interested in her, he had made her interested in him. They had talked around a dozen topics and she could think of a hundred more that she would enjoy exploring with him. Never had she so appreciated a man's company.

"Do you have a music player in this White House home of yours?"

"Uh, sort of. I have a speaker system in the other room that I can drop my iPod into. But it's loaded with lectures on governance, international law, documents I don't have time to read unless I'm exercising or something. That sort of thing."

"Show me." She stood and waited for him to gain his feet. He sounded as compulsive as she was. Her own playlist included the complete recordings of the latest World Heritage Conservation Conference with a special focus on overly-rapid urban development and its effect on the present sites. She'd only heard the sessions at which she'd spoken or been on a panel, now she was trying to catch up with all of the other tracks.

But she did have one other thing stored there.

He led her across the Central Hall. Their Scrabble set had been cleaned up, though the board still remained on the low table from the prior night, as if awaiting another game. Another time perhaps. Directly opposite the kitchen was a small living room. Well, small in comparison to the vast expanse of the hall. Two sofas, several armchairs, a pair of low tables scattered with magazines and file folders. A space shoved clear where he was obviously used to dining when eating alone. It had been decorated in dark greens with a tasteful eye.

"The previous First Lady," he remarked, noticing her attention. "Not my wife. Not my former wife, er, deceased wife. She decorated this room for her husband. I liked it and made Katherine leave it alone when she was doing the rest of the Residence."

"It looks comfortable, and very masculine."

"If that's an ego stroke, I'll take it. If patronizing, I'll ignore it. There's the player, but it doesn't even have radio."

She'd retrieved her purse as they passed through the hall and she fished out her iPod. Plugging it in, she found what she was looking for and pressed Play.

Genny set aside her purse and moved to stand before the President. "It is not the best music for a first dance together, but perhaps it is good nonetheless."

A Christmas carol came out of the speakers.

# # #

Geneviève moved into his arms. Peter didn't know what to do with the surge of energy that coursed through his body. Other than when he'd taken her hand to help her out of The Beast and the briefest of kisses last night, they had barely touched. He didn't count her hand tucked in the crook of his elbow.

Well, okay, he had counted it, until he suddenly had his arms full of luscious woman.

Her idea of dancing was not some stand-offish American form of dance. It wasn't even a waltz distance. She simply filled his arms.

She placed a hand around his back and her cheek on his shoulder. With no other choice, he tentatively slid his hands around her waist. Never had he felt such a thing. "Thing," there was a good word. Mr. Scrabble King had just lost his all his words.

Geneviève began a slow shuffle to some song he couldn't make heads or tails of. Not because it was unfamiliar, but because he didn't have sufficient attention span to identify what he was hearing.

The scent of her filled him as much as her warmth. She wasn't that much shorter than he was, so her head on his shoulder nestled up against his neck.

"Hmm, you are smelling very good."

He couldn't have said it better. "I took a shower."

Her laugh was soft and welcoming.

Then he lay his cheek on her hair. It was even softer and thicker than it looked. It was impossible to tell when he first came in contact with it. He brushed a hand over its length, and down onto her back. He stroked it again, pulling some of it aside so that her face would not be lost in it.

"I know, I need to cut it off. I just never get around to it."

"If you ever do that, I will immediately cancel your visa to our country."

"Hmm," it was practically a purr of satisfaction.

He could feel the sound ripple from her chest to his.

"You certainly know how to make a girl feel welcome."

All he could think about was his need to kiss this woman. And then it struck him that if she weren't willing, anticipating just that, she'd not be in his arms.

Sometimes he was a little stupid, but that didn't mean he was slow once he figured out what was going on.

# # #

Genny sighed with pleasure as he kissed her. She'd wanted it to be his choice. She'd wanted it to be his choice during dinner, and before that in the museum. Truth be told, she'd wanted it to be his choice since that very first chance meeting at the U.N. in the Dag Hammarskjöld Library six months before. Though she'd have laughed at anyone who had told her so at the time.

She didn't need a man. Her life was too full. Her last lover had been Klaus. He had been a good lover, right until she was named Chief of Unit for Southeast Asia World Heritage and he was passed over as Assistant Chief of Northern Africa. Then he had been not so good.

Perhaps the President would be her next lover. The way he kissed her made that a definite possibility. He might be a world leader, but he also smelled and felt wonderful. He held her with a gentleness of wonder. Did he also possess an animal side hiding down behind all of those defenses that were ever so polite and ever so careful?

For she could see his defenses as clearly as she could feel his lips searing against hers. That had been clear to her from the first moment of their meeting. He hid behind layers of hurt, of Scrabble games and ex-wives, of his past and most definitely of his job. Well, she might as well start there before his kiss melted her into an absolute puddle.

She broke the kiss and snuggled back against him as they moved softly to a slow rendition of *Have Yourself a Merry Little Christmas*.

"So, Mr. President, do you have a bedroom nearby as well?"

He laughed, a delightful sound that rumbled against her ear. "How can you ask that question and still not call me by my Christian name?"

Genny pulled back as if in surprise and looked up at him from the circle of his arms. "Oh, Mr. President, this isn't about you. This is about the most powerful leader in the world."

"So, if I lose my next election in two years, it will be over between us?"

"*Absolument!*" With a sly smile, she crossed her fingers and spit over them, a child's promise. "It is only the President I want to be making love to."

He scooped her up in his arms and moved toward a side door. "I'd better win the next goddamn election, that's all I have to say."

In the darkened bedroom, he began to undress her to Handel's *Hallelujah Chorus*.

Chapter 5

Genny was going to miss her luncheon meeting at the U.N. and she didn't care in the slightest. *Merde!* The way she felt, she didn't care if she never moved again. The room was dark, but the man beside her was moving. "Where are you going?"

"Good morning. I was trying to leave without waking you."

"Oh, you are the love them and leave their bed in the middle of the night sort of President."

"No. First, you're in my bed, not the other way around. Second, I have a job."

"As do I. So, you are saying that you would leave your bed without even kissing the woman in it?"

"I can't even see where you are."

"Turn on the light." While he fumbled for a moment to do so, she pushed down the covers she'd been so comfortably ensconced in a moment before.

"There. I—" He turned to face her even as she blinked hard against the brightness. "Holy shit!"

"What is 'Holy shit!'?"

"You are!"

Genny had meant to tease him, but his reply was so emphatic. She squeezed open one eye enough to see that he was sitting up, his feet off the other side of the bed, and gaping at her over his shoulder.

45

Though they had made love in the shadows of what little light washed in from the living room, she had known he had a good body. He had proved it many times throughout the night. But now that the light was on, she could see that the definition of it wasn't merely tactile. He really looked wonderful.

She especially liked the look of total shock on his face as he inspected her body. Inspected? Not the right verb. Perhaps 'devoured with his eyes' was better. She felt last night's heat slowly rekindling deep within her, a heat that he had stoked far past any level she had ever known.

"Why aren't you a model or something?" His voice was breathless.

"Because then I would not have ended up in your bed and we would not have had last night."

"Okay, you win that one." He reached out a hand, so tentatively it almost hurt to watch.

She finally took his wrist to pull his hand towards her.

Rather than reaching for her body, he stroked her cheek and down her arm.

"Did she hurt you so much? This dead wife of yours? That you are afraid to touch me."

Peter startled and his gaze jumped to hers.

"It is written on you, my lover. You think that you have secrets from a woman who has done what we did last night? *Non!* You do not, so you may let that go, Mr. President."

He opened his mouth to speak, once, twice, three times. Then he burst out. "I have never met a woman like you, Kim-Ly Geneviève Beauchamp." Then his kiss stopped any reply she might have made. A kiss that he didn't release until he had once more driven them both up and over heights that she had never imagined possible.

He collapsed back into sleep, his exhaustion overcoming the four a.m. time on his clock. Her leg across his hips and her head cradled on his shoulder were not enough to keep him awake.

A job where the man must work so hard was not a good thing. But what he did at his job was a good thing. It was a strange contrast.

Genny slowly traced a hand over his chest, feeling the even rise and fall of his breathing. His heartbeat, a soft song in her ear.

She knew she was in trouble as she lay upon him and sleep eluded her. She closed her eyes and relished once more the warmth and strength of him. As if he could conquer the world. As if she could too for simply being with him.

Then she spoke words that she knew she would wish to take back some day. Words that left a mark upon her that she swore no man ever would again.

"I have never met anyone like you, Mr. President."

# # #

The phone blasted Peter awake. He grabbed it out of an instinct of self-preservation. At that volume, another ring might kill him. He was a very heavy sleeper and it took a very loud sound to awaken him. But it made the second ring hell.

"Uh," was all he managed. The clock read five a.m. Normal call. No need to panic.

"Good morning, Mr. President." Daniel. "Time to get up. Also, I was going to drop off some papers on my way to the office, some things I think we could review over breakfast."

"Uh, sure, I…" He trailed off as a vision walked around from the other side of his bed. Clothed in nothing but a tiny silver medallion at her neck, she looked like a goddess walking upon the newborn world. Geneviève strode across his bedroom carpet long, lean, and golden with a confidence most women couldn't muster in a thousand-dollar power suit. Her hair even billowed as she moved. She disappeared into his bathroom. He hoped to god he wasn't hallucinating.

"Sir?" Daniel's question buzzed in Peter's ear.

"Sorry. Let's, uh, not do that today."

"Absolutely, sir. I'll see you in the office."

"Wait! Daniel?"

"Sir?"

"Could you have someone fetch Ms. Beauchamp's clothes and other belongings from the Hay-Adams?"

"I'll, uh, see to it, sir. And may I say, about time, Mr. President. I've only been hearing about her for six months."

"Go to hell, Daniel."

"After you, sir."

Peter may or may not have hung up the phone. His next clear thought was leaning against the door jamb and watching Geneviève stepping into his shower. A simple, ordinary movement that might occur a thousand times in a couple's life. It fired both his body and his imagination.

It had been but a single night, but she made him want ten thousand more.

# # #

"I swear that I'm not stalking you. I simply forgot today's schedule."

"There are many coincidences in your life, Mr. President."

"And still it's 'Mr. President!'" Peter faced a highly skeptical Geneviève across the island in the kitchen where he'd had dinner removed and breakfast delivered while they showered. On finding that her suitcase was soon to arrive, she had wrapped herself in his terrycloth bathrobe and nothing else. Katherine would have had on a nightgown, underwear, slippers, makeup, and who knew what else.

Geneviève wore only his bathrobe; her hair still hung wet down her back. He couldn't tell if she was angry or suspicious or quite what she was feeling. Like last night, she was several steps ahead of him and he trailed far behind.

"I have a luncheon speech at the Eastern Governors Association Conference in New York. Then several meetings on Wall Street this afternoon. So, I'd be glad to give you a ride to Manhattan."

"And what will your press think when I come out of the White House with my suitcase and climb aboard your Marine One helicopter? What then, Mr. President?" She crossed her arms over her chest.

"They'd think I was just about the luckiest man on the planet."

He could see her gathering for the next round of protest. Couldn't the woman just take a compliment and be happy about it? No. She was as tenacious as he was. Though he did seriously like the image of them as a couple.

"Yes, Geneviève, I know all of the arguments. Trust me on that. The President's private life is anything but private. So, I must live at least part of my private life in public. If you don't choose to, I understand *absolument*. I am glad to have you escorted out through the Treasury Building garage and delivered wherever you would like to go. We can try to keep it as quiet and private as we can. Frankly, I wouldn't blame you for running in the other direction entirely, though I truly hope that you won't."

She was listening. She wasn't raging or interrupting or jumping ahead. She was actually allowing him to speak his piece. And he'd wager a fifty-point headstart for their next Scrabble game that it wasn't because he was President. This was simply how she would be in a relationship, a startling concept in itself. Her simply treating him as if his thoughts had value evoked an answer that was surprising even to him. He didn't speak from what he thought, but rather what he felt.

"I want to be with you. I want to see where this can go. We can keep that as private as possible, or we can be ourselves in public and damn the press. I assure you that little of my own life remains private, but I'm willing to try if you want."

"You want to see me again?" Her voice was suddenly soft. Her arms remained folded across her chest and she sat still as a marble statue on the kitchen stool ignoring her half-eaten waffle and the coffee she had declared as "too weak except for small children."

Peter looked at the ceiling, but found no guidance there to understanding this woman. One moment she was worried about the appearances of his presidency and the next moment she was shocked that this wasn't a one-night stand.

When he looked back at her, it was as if she'd changed, though she hadn't moved a muscle. He could now see that her arms weren't crossed in anger, but rather wrapped about herself for protection. Her caution wasn't just for his presidency, but for herself as well. A vulnerable Geneviève Beauchamp was something he hadn't expected.

He didn't know what to say to her, how to reassure her when he was sure of so little himself.

So, instead, he stepped around the island and simply enfolded her into his arms.

She didn't unclench her own arms. She just leaned her face into his chest and let herself be held. Geneviève wasn't crying, but he could feel her dragging in deep breaths.

It took a while, but she slowly relaxed until she lay against him, rather than just being held, and her shoulders softened beneath his gentle strokes. Finally she sighed deeply and appeared to fully let go.

"As Christ is my witness," her voice was rough, almost harsh. "You had better be worth it, Mr. President. You are making my heart in danger."

Chapter 6

G*enny had spent the* morning alone in the Residence. Being alone, the first thing she'd did was her daily workout of stretches, techniques, and *kata*. Because she'd missed yesterday, she pushed for over an hour until she'd needed another shower. Then she'd worked on catching up on e-mails and trying not to feel self conscious about being in Peter's home when he wasn't. She'd started in his Living Room, but moved to the Central Hall. Even that was too personal, but she was unsure where else to go. He was taking a series of morning meetings in the West Wing before their flight.

Their flight.

Just minutes from now they'd be declaring to the world that they were seeing each other. Dating. Sleeping together. That didn't bother her overly much. What other people thought about them being a couple was not her concern, what they thought was their own problem.

What was different about this public declaration was the impact on herself. It wasn't that she'd taken a new lover, they came and they went, not often, but it was part of the cycle of a healthy life. But to be dating the President, that was a more definitive statement, made more real by his office and his importance to the world at large. Such a thing meant that more thought and consideration had been given to the matter than someone you met at a conference and liked.

Peter Matthews had topped the most-eligible bachelor list for the two years since his wife's death. Of course, Prince William had been married by then. Young Harry, now fourth in line to the British throne, had only placed a distant second.

Even that was not the matter. It was how she felt around Peter. She had never been so comfortable except in her own home. She'd had lovers who were casual about nudity in the home, but she had never so enjoyed walking in front of a powerful and erudite man and striking him speechless. And how could such a man know her so perfectly that he spoke not a word when the nerves overwhelmed her, but simply cradled her until she could want to be nowhere else.

He was maddening, frustrating, beautiful, and kind. He was also almost as afraid of intimacy as she was. Not physical intimacy. That was clearly not a problem between them They had found such joy in each other's bodies that it was hard to credit. Even thinking of him caused her pulse to rise and bring a flush to her cheeks, despite the e-mail she was writing to her Assistant Unit Chief regarding how to gracefully accept a keynote speaker position for a major conference that she had already said she wouldn't be attending as a participant.

She and Peter hadn't been like two teenagers gone wild with hormones, nor had they been like two adults enjoying a good round of casual sex. They had made love as if each moment were a new discovery to be cherished and remembered. It overshadowed all her past experiences.

That was the intimacy that he brought to their relationship, unexpectedly and not entirely welcome. She knew this man. Not his past, there had been so little time for that. But she knew him nonetheless. As if he had slipped a piece of her heart into clearer view than it had ever been.

He did that to her. President Peter Matthews overshadowed all her experiences of men, and he had done it in only two days. How could she account for this to herself? It was impossible for a relationship to be built on such a narrow pedestal, and yet it felt as stable as the Borobudur Temple which had survived fifteen-hundred years despite jungle growth, being buried in volcanic ash, ever-chaotic Indonesian politics, and even extremists' bombs.

"Are you ready?"

Genny startled and looked up to see the same Secret Service agent standing nearby. She hadn't heard the woman's approach. She packed away her laptop and turned to make a quick survey, nothing left behind her. Just her suitcase and cross-shoulder bag that held her purse and computer.

The agent led her toward the elevator. "Sorry about not offering to carry your bags, ma'am. But I need to keep my hands free."

"It was not expected that you would do so. So, are you assigned to me?"

They traveled together down the long hall on the White House Ground Floor. Here the Christmas décor was more subdued than elsewhere. This corridor was only traversed by servants and by those from the West Wing with business in the Residence. There were no public tours here, and it felt more normal.

"I am, ma'am. For as…" She ended awkwardly.

"For as long as I am dating your President. I understand. Then you should call me Genny."

"That wouldn't be proper, Ms. Beauchamp." She held open a door and guided Genny through the Palm Room and outside along the Colonnade that led toward the West Wing.

"And why do we women care about such things as being proper? That is for the men to care about."

The agent stopped for a moment, just feet from a Marine guard at a glass door. At a glass door in a wall that curved.

Genny took a deep breath. The Oval Office was through that door. She had best make herself ready. It gave her more nerves than the first time she'd entered the U.N. Security Council Chamber to address the council.

The agent held out a hand. "Beatrice, most call me Beat."

"Beat, that is your agent name. Beatrice, that is what I shall call you. Me you shall call Genny." They shook hands and Genny took a deep breath and held it before nodding for Beatrice to lead the way.

The agent held open the door, let her through, and then let it close remaining outside. Leaving Genny to face the Oval Office on her own.

# # #

Peter was just finishing up with Daniel on the latest budget proposal from the National Science Foundation for next year's Arctic and Antarctic research when the door opened off to his right.

By the time he was able to glance over, Genny's face was turning bright red.

"Breathe, Geneviève! Breathe!" he called out as he went to her.

She blew out a breath, gulped in another, then managed little more than a squeak, "I can't, Mr. President. I just can't!"

He placed an arm around her shoulders and pulled her into the room. "I know. I know. I had the same problem. Sometimes I still do, so many great Presidents have walked here before me."

"Me too, Genny," Daniel offered cheerily as he gathered up the paperwork from the Resolute Desk. "First time I was actually in the room was for the interview that led to me being Chief of Staff. So scared you could hear my knees knocking clear back to Tennessee."

She blew out a breath again, loudly, and slowly her normal color began coming back.

"We should make love here, Mr. President."

"Whoops! I'm gone." Daniel practically sprinted for the door. Traitor.

"Uh, I don't think that even I have the nerve to do that, Geneviève."

"I'm not suggesting one of Jack Kennedy's naked coed pool parties, or that you smuggle me into your room like FDR did. I merely suggest that you and I should make love here."

"You're serious?"

"Well, I think it would be good for you. This is the center of your power, this oval room. And...," she abruptly blew out a final breath and laughed a little shakily. "But I think I agree with you. I would not have the nerve to make love in such a place."

A secretary breezed in through one of the doors. "Here's your speech and your coat, Mr. President." She held it open for him to slip on.

"Thanks, Jasmine," he turned his attention back to Geneviève. "Besides, there's a couple problems. For one thing, the doors don't lock."

Jasmine's sudden backward glance told him that he should have waited a moment longer before speaking. He almost called her back in to explain that they were joking, like that sounded believable. He let her go.

"That is why you have guards," Geneviève was studying the several doors that the room boasted.

"Well," he turned her by the shoulders to look at the bay window facing the broad South Lawn. "The guards also stand outside the glass on this side."

"So, tell them not to peek. We will turn out the lights. I will promise not to cry out too loud no matter how much you make me want to." Now she was clearly teasing him, her hand patting his cheek, placing a small kiss on his cheek.

"I am not having this conversation. I am not standing in the Oval Office and having this conversation." He checked the portfolio Jasmine had handed him to make sure she'd also included his schedule and the notes for the other meetings.

"What? You think that others have not been here and made love to their women in this place? If so, you are a big fool, Mr. President."

Peter glanced up at the portraits of Washington, Lincoln, and Kennedy hanging from the office walls. Kennedy definitely. Grant maybe. And…

"I am not having this conversation."

"How do you feel about kissing a woman in the Oval Office? Because I feel as if I am about to fly apart."

"I think I can accede to that demand at least." And before she could respond and make him even crazier, he swept her into his arms. She grabbed onto his coat's lapels and hung on.

Then he guided her toward the door she had just entered.

Great. Just great.

The image of her languishing naked and sweaty upon the Oval Office rug was now firmly lodged in his brain, and he knew it would remain there for as long as he served as President.

Chapter 7

*G*enny *wasn't quite sure* how it happened.

Perhaps it was because the President was a sneaky, manipulative, tricky man. Perhaps it was because she was a wanton, lustful wench utterly beguiled by America's leader. Or perhaps it was just because he had asked so nicely and she couldn't resist him.

She was climbing out of the Beatrice's car and once again entering the White House just five days after she'd left it on the Marine One helicopter. Genny couldn't have come sooner, as she'd just had three days of meetings in Paris before returning to New York. She hadn't even slept, merely spent three hours in the office before hopping the train down to D.C.

"It's cookie night," Peter had said. "You can't miss cookie night. We'll wait until Friday night for you, but not longer."

So, here she was for cookie night, whatever that was. It was five o'clock local time, making it eleven at night in Paris. But she hadn't really had time to adapt, so she figured her body time was probably somewhere around the mid-Atlantic Oceanic Ridge. Lost in deep water far from any shore.

A butler appeared and collected her suitcase and coat, saying that he would place them in the Residence for when she needed them. "The President and Dr. Darlington are still in the Oval Office. Would you care to join them there or wait in the Residence?"

She opted for the Oval Office and Beatrice led her away. Partly, she wanted to see if she had adapted to the room at all, but mostly she wanted to see Peter.

Even when married to Gérard, she thought nothing of traveling weeks at a time away from home. Perhaps she laid too much of the failure of their marriage at his feet. Yes, he was an arrogant Frenchman with such an insular view of the civilized world that he was practically American about it. But neither had she been the easiest person to live with.

Peter Matthews however, was making her want to be with him. Two evenings and one night together and she missed the man after only five days. Damn him! Even worse, she'd missed him the minute they'd driven in opposite directions from the Manhattan Downtown Heliport.

The Oval Office had not decreased its impact in the slightest. Peter waved her in and continued listening to whatever phone conversation he was having. She passed by his chair and planted a kiss on top of his head. It was only as she stepped by, that the gesture struck her. How many times had she seen her mother do that same thing on her father's head when he would come home and dropped with relief into his big armchair, glad to be among his family once again.

This was a little different in that the next moment Peter clearly cut off the other speaker. "Mr. Prime Minister, I'm telling you very simply, that if Israel takes such an action it will be without the support of the U.S. Not militarily, financially, or politically. If the U.N. court wants to take you down for that, they will have a hundred percent support of the Unites States Government. Do I make myself clear?"

Okay, maybe it was a lot different. But it had felt the same, a casual, easy acknowledgement that she was glad to see him. She did her best not to pay attention to the abruptly altered tone of the conversation as Israel abruptly tried to placate its primary ally. Instead, she turned to inspect the room.

Perhaps she was adapting to the room. This time she could see more detail. A Christmas tree, the three-meter baby brother of the ten-meter monster on the Ellipse, it had also been lit in a cheerful and bright imitation of the American flag. A few presents were scattered about the base, she glanced down, from the President to his staff by the labels.

"I don't let them buy presents for me," Peter slid up behind her and wrapped his arms around her waist. He nuzzled her neck in greeting. "I don't want them to be uncomfortable trying to decide what to give me."

"What do you give to them?"

"Oh, illegal land grants, major tax concessions. Have you met Felicia, cute little African woman who is also a fabulous speech writer? She asked for a bomb strike for Christmas, something to do with an ex-husband. Things like that."

"I like the way she thinks."

"Maybe I should get one for all the women of America. Really tie up the women's vote for the next election."

"Yes, and it would also drop the population of your country by about a half."

"I'd win the women by a landslide that way. Of course, just to be fair, I'd have to offer the services of the Special Forces to the men. No, the whole thing could get too messy and depopulate my constituency entirely, then there'd be no one to vote for me. I talked her into accepting a small Caribbean island just as soon as the Caribbeans are done with it."

Genny stepped away from him, waved to Mr. Lincoln, who didn't glower one bit less despite the gesture, and continued her tour of the room. It was startling in its simplicity. The three grand portraits were each framed by a pair of holly wreaths bearing large red ribbons. A fire crackled happily in a marble fireplace at the far end of the Oval Office. On the mantle above it were obviously the family heirloom decorations. Old sleigh bells, nicked candy cane candles, a slightly battered set of reindeer in a smoke-stained candelabra, and a small knit Santa who slouched against the wall. She straightened the Santa who was in danger of tipping over onto an alarmed looking ceramic gnome.

At the small tables among the seating in the center of the room, more gnomes cheerfully offered ceramic bags overflowing with chocolates. She took one and bit into it.

"Oh my god, that's so good," dark chocolate with a Grand Marnier truffle interior. "That's as good as sex."

"I hope not, or I've been doing something wrong." Peter had remained by the tree and watched her inspection, hands slid comfortably into the pockets of his navy-blue slacks. His tie, something in Christmasy colors, hung slightly loosened about his neck. The white linen shirt made him look clean, no, pure. As if he were the purest version of himself while standing there watching her.

She moved back to him. And could now see his tie, sporting a team of Santas facing off in a hockey game against some very determined looking elves. Genny rested her palm on the center of his ridiculous tie and his wonderful chest.

"You, my lover Mr. President, are doing absolutely nothing wrong in that area. Someone trained you so very well on how to please a woman in your bed."

"You did."

"*Moi?*"

"*Tu.* I simply imagined everything I could do to make you happy and did that. You inspire me. In many ways." He said the last on a drifting voice, half to himself.

"You must stop this, Mr. President." Genny was having difficulty breathing. Each time he said something like that to her, he shifted her self-image.

"Stop what?"

"Your flattery." It made her feel as if she was more than she knew she was.

"It's working, is it? Cool!"

"Ugh. You are such a man. Now kiss me like you have been imagining since I arrived."

"You mean since the moment you left?"

Genny dragged his face to hers and kissed him before he could say more. He was going to kill her yet. Or slay her heart which, for the first time, she thought might be even worse.

# # #

"So, what is this cookie night?" Genny and the President waited in the Dining Hall of the Second Floor of the Residence. It was so formal, like everything else here. White wainscoting, elegantly tasteful wallpaper the color of a soft sunrise, and an elaborate crystal chandelier dangling over a circular table of dark mahogany that could seat ten. And the seam down the middle suggested that it could be expanded for even more. A spread of hors d'oeuvres had been spread upon the table. She took a few on a small plate. Peter, refusing to cave to the formality of his surroundings, grazed, taking an olive here, a deviled egg there, and eating them with little regard if they were to scatter crumbs.

Per instruction, she had changed into casual clothes, at least the most casual she had with her, black slacks and turtleneck. Peter wore jeans and a flannel shirt open at the collar with the sleeves rolled up. He looked comfortable, at home in this crazy house of the American President.

"You'll just have to wait and see. Besides, it's Daniel's thing, so we have to wait for him and a couple of others to join us. Oh, I should mention— Oh, here's Em."

Emily Beale stepped into the room. "Mark bagged out on us," she said by way of introduction.

Not even a hello, as if Genny were simply a member of the family, expected rather than merely welcome. It was a nice gesture. She hoped that's all it was because otherwise she'd start to overthink how it felt to be here.

"Mark does that whenever I mention anything about a kitchen other than eating in one. I swear, the only place he'll cook is if we have a campfire and he just caught the trout. He made some lousy excuse just because we are shipping out on a training exercise tomorrow, as if that were something new."

"What you should do," Genny glanced sidelong at Peter to make sure he was listening. She decided to see just how much she could tease him, "is exactly what I plan to do with this Mr. President. Our first house," the President suddenly had a strangled look on his face as if he were choking on his own breath. Perfect. That would teach him to have secrets from her.

"It will have no kitchen. I will install an enormous American barbeque and make him always do the cooking for me."

Emily idly thudded Peter on the back with one hand to restart his breathing, hard enough to nearly drive him onto the table, while considering Genny.

"You're smart. I should have known you would be, since Peter picked you out of the crowd. I just might do that." Her smile lit her eyes more brightly than laughter ever could.

Before Peter had fully recovered, Daniel and his wife Alice arrived from the floor above. He carried a small sheaf of papers and index cards. These looked worn and tattered, oddly out of place in the White House. Something so simple brought to the eye the museum-like perfection of every adornment here, making the whole of it suddenly appear false.

Another couple arrived close behind them, an older couple that she didn't recognize. The attractive woman wore a short bob of graying hair that might have once been blond, a cashmere sweater and perfectly tailored jeans. The man was balding, dressed casually, and looked like an older version of—

"There they are. Hey Mom! Dad!"

Peter traded quick hugs with them as Genny felt all of the blood drain out of her body. It was a setup and she was the pretty woman suddenly on display.

"Please allow me to introduce you. Geneviève, this is Randolph, former Senate Majority leader, retired, so thank God I don't have to deal with him. And Gloria. She's still a U.S. Court of Appeals Circuit Judge. Mom, Dad, this is—"

"We know who she is, you idiot." His mother's verbal slap brought Peter's words to an abrupt halt.

Gloria held onto Genny's hand which was good, for it was about the only thing that kept her from flattening Peter onto the hardwood floor. And she was going to make sure it hurt on the way down, because the Secret Service was probably going to shoot her before she'd have a chance to finish him off.

"I can't believe he didn't tell you we were invited," Gloria rested her other hand over Genny's, as if she knew she were enhancing the longevity of her son's existence by doing so. "There are some things about which he is remarkably stupid. I, for one, am pleased to meet you. After I saw the pictures in the news, because of course he doesn't even think to call his mother, I googled you. You are a very impressive young woman, perhaps you can keep him in line."

"Perhaps I can practice my martial arts sparring techniques upon him. Hard." Genny finally managed to shift her gaze over to Peter. He looked as if he understood that this was not a good surprise.

Randolph cuffed his son smartly on the back of the head, which made Genny feel a little better.

#

"It's an old family tradition," Daniel was spreading out his precious recipes on the table.

Peter had tried to get to Geneviève a couple of times, but she was clearly avoiding him. Every time he turned, she was on the opposite side of his mother or father. Even Alice and Em were putting up subtle barricades around her. He couldn't seem to get to her.

"We've always made cookie boxes for any family who couldn't be home for Christmas. I first thought, for this year, we could make some for our own families."

Peter tried to catch Geneviève's attention so that he could signal her to retire with him for a moment to the hallway to explain, but she wouldn't even look at him.

"But that would only be for me and Mark. Plus some extras for Emily to take to her parents here in town. Genny, I don't know if you have family."

"I do. In Vietnam."

"Good," Daniel continued as if there were no problem at all. Usually his Chief of Staff helped him muddle through situations, just as he'd helped some with Daniel's courtship of Alice. Right at the moment he was being completely useless.

"So that would make three boxes of cookies, not very ambitious. But I thought we should spread it wider. I think we should make as many boxes as we can, and send them out to the kids living in shelters in D.C. Cookies not made by the White House chefs, but by us personally."

"What a wonderful idea," everyone was agreeing and turning to inspect the recipes.

Peter tried to move in beside Geneviève and received a sharp elbow to the gut that hurt and forced him to back off.

"Okay! I screwed up! I'm sorry!" At his outburst, everybody turned to stare at him. Everybody except Geneviève.

He took her elbow and turned her gently until she faced him.

Her glare and the hurt was not a pretty expression on her face and he was sorry he'd put it there.

"I'm sorry. I didn't know if Mom and Dad could make it when I invited you."

"When you found out, you could have called me." Her voice was neither hot nor tear-choked as he'd expected. It sounded cold, and dangerous.

"I could have, if you'd given me your goddamned phone number." He knew he should be the one keeping his temper. He always did, in every situation. But his need for her, to be with her, was driving him near to madness.

Geneviève remained perfectly steady, not even needing to cross her arms in front of her to fend him off. "And your Secret Service doesn't have my number?"

"Of course they do, at least I assume so. But I didn't want to ask them. I have already made it so that your life is smeared across the front pages of the news, I wanted to leave you some privacy."

Was her look softening? He couldn't tell.

"And why didn't you tell me when I arrived?" Her demand sounded no softer. "I have been here over thirty minutes. Long enough for you to kiss me in the Oval Office. Long enough to try to drag me into your bed when we changed clothes though you said we would be late if you did."

Okay, now he was the one who didn't want to meet her eyes. Even less though, did he want to see the eyes of anyone else in the room. No one, not even his own parents, had the decency to make even the least gesture toward leaving, they all were too fascinated by the goings on here.

So, this too would be public.

He took her hands in his. They didn't grasp, but neither did she pull them away.

"Kim-Ly Geneviève Beauchamp, you consume me. You make me think of nothing but you, every moment you are with me. I forgot that I hadn't told you my parents would be here, because I was too busy being happy." Then he waited. Waited while the woman with the greenest eyes he'd ever seen inspected him and decided her verdict.

Then, when he thought he might pass out from holding his breath, she stepped forward and kissed him on each cheek. He half feared that she was saying goodbye, until she kissed him lightly on the mouth, as lightly as that first kiss. Pulling him close against her by the strong grasp of their hands, she laid her cheek on his and whispered in his ear.

"I was right, you are making my heart in such danger."

Peter freed his hands, wrapped his arms around her, and simply tried to hold on.

His mother and Alice were crying, not even attempting to mop their cheeks. Even Em was looking pretty sniffly which was hard to imagine. His Dad thumped him on the back, though not hard enough to disturb the woman nestled in his arms.

Daniel just gave him a sharp nod of approval, as if he'd known all along it would be okay. Then he spoke loudly.

"So, about these cookies."

Everyone laughed and turned back to the task at hand.

He stayed close by Geneviève. If he was putting her heart "in such danger," what in the world was she doing to his? Making it pound until he couldn't hear a single thing anyone said. It pounded so hard that it set up echoes that would never stop, not until they were buried deep in his soul.

# # #

"There are no French-style cookies here," Genny inspected Daniel's recipe collection. "No dessert from Vietnam. I cannot send a Christmas box to my family without these ingredients."

"I have this," Daniel offered her a recipe for Sienese *Pan Forte.*

"That is Italian."

"I know how to make a decent custard," Emily offered.

"Oh, and that will ship well in a cookie box."

Emily looked chagrined, "Oh, right."

"I will need some ingredients." She did her best to maintain the appearance of calm. The pressure had eased in the room. And it had eased in her heart, in one way.

"We can dial down to the main White House kitchen for almost anything we need. They'll send it up on the elevator." Daniel pointed to a tall, but narrow steel door in the corner that Genny hadn't noticed.

She began making a list.

"Hey, I thought you said you didn't know how to cook?"

"This is not cooking, Mr. President. This is baking. Even more important, this is Christmas baking. That I know how to do." She focused on finishing her list so that she appeared busy.

For the pressure on her heart had not eased. In less than a week, she had fallen in love with a man, and she had only come to understand that in the last minute or two. It was not something she did easily. Or at all, in her memory. She had thought she loved Gérard, or she wouldn't have married him. But it had felt nothing like this. Nothing like when Peter had faced her and told her that she consumed his thoughts.

From another man, that would be lust. But this was not a normal man. This was one of the most powerful thinkers on the planet. And as, she knew by what he'd achieved already in his Presidency, a very smart and determined man. That her mere presence could distract him into indiscretions and poor communication spoke of far more than it would have in any other man. He had just laid his heart out on the table in front of his friends and parents for all to see. And he had offered it to her.

Whether or not he understood what he had done, she did. And how could she not be swept away by such a revelation?

"There," she finished her list. Her throat was tight and she was glad to find Emily close beside her. The woman leaned in to look at the list, and ever so casually draped an arm across Genny's shoulders. With no one the wiser, the woman hugged her. Clearly she too had seen what Peter, her childhood friend, did not yet realize.

"Interesting looking ingredients, what do they make?"

"This," Genny indicated the first column. "Will make a *Nougat Noir au Miel*. It is a dark, what would you call, caramel of lavender honey with almonds. It goes between wafer paper if they have it, or dusted confectioners sugar if they do not. And this a *Nougat Blanc,* a white sugar and pistachio nut candy. Both very traditional French. They are the black and the white, the bad boy and the good girl of Santa's Christmas list, or so my mother always called them."

"That definitely works for me," Emily looked up at the President. "Bad Boy, Peter. Bad Boy! Coal in your stocking."

"Could I get that dark caramel thing instead? Sounds good."

"Only," Genny looked up at him, the first time she had dared to face him since his confession. "If you promise me one thing."

"Anything." His statement was so emphatic that it set her back for a moment more. He might truly mean that in more ways than he knew. She needed something light and funny. Something to stop the fluttering he was causing in her chest.

"You must promise me, Mr. President. That the next time you have personal news, you will call your parents."

Everyone laughed. Gloria actually applauded and Randolph slapped his son on the back.

But Peter looked at her as if she'd said something else entirely. His gaze spoke of just what reason he might have for calling his parents in the near future.

It was not possible that she had just spoken of becoming engaged to the President.

# # #

They had baked and laughed and drunk wine and eaten cookies and relaxed more that evening than Peter had done in a long time. The kitchen was comfortably sized, but with seven cooks, there had been a constant friendly jostling for prime counter space.

Sheets and sheets of cookies had gone through the oven, overspilling the kitchen counters and even the big Dining Room table. More coffee tables had been recruited from the Central Hall, dragged in and covered with paper boxes. They'd lined each box, the size to hold a ream of paper, with red tissue paper, then filled them with a wide variety of cookies, and tied them closed with red and green ribbons.

Some monster chocolate chip that Daniel called a Paul Bunyan Molasses cookie. Narrow slices of Em's decadent *Pan Forte* and her chocolate-dipped macaroons. His mom's Cinnamon-Raisin Biscotti. As a group they tackled several of Daniel's recipes. They'd made Ginger-Squared Squares, which included both fresh-grated and candied ginger in square oatmeal bars. Alice had contributed a Cream Cheese Cranberry Curl that she called C-to-the-fourth. In addition to the nougats, Geneviève had made something she called Ginger Jam. Starting with three kilos of ginger root, she had peeled and sliced and boiled and mixed like a madwoman, ultimately creating a Vietnamese ginger candy similar to flattened jellybeans that no one could stop eating. And everyone had worked on the mounds of cut-out sugar cookies in the shapes of Santas, reindeers, and Christmas trees all decorated with colored royal icing.

They trashed the kitchen.

Their hands were stained with food dye. Their clothes powdered with flour and sugar despite the aprons his mother had handed out. The entire residence had smelled heavenly.

And each time Peter found himself working shoulder-to-shoulder with Geneviève it was as if his world went quiet. It was simply where they belonged—close, comfortable, easy together. He knew he was being stupid, but there was no doubt what they had said to each other across the Dining Room without a word spoken. He knew as well as she did that they had each said the impossible.

They could both imagine being married some day.

The logistics of how they could even live together was beyond imagining; their lives, their worlds were different. But for this woman, he could easily imagine spending the rest of his years finding ways of making her happy.

It was well past midnight when they stumbled into his bedroom. She mumbled something about her body being on Paris time and he suddenly felt guilty. It was seven or eight a.m. her time. By the time he'd brushed his teeth, she was crashed down atop the covers.

She barely woke as he undressed her and tucked her beneath the covers, smoothing back the hair off her face. He sat on the edge of the bed and simply watched her sleep for the longest time.

Geneviève had not only won the sincere friendship of his parents, but she had also drawn Em's clear stamp of approval. Of all the people in Peter's life, no one knew him better. Though she'd been six years younger, they had still been best friends growing up, the impossibly precocious little girl next door. Their lives had gone separate directions, more his fault than hers, until two years ago when she'd stepped back into the President's world as a Captain of the U.S. Army Special Forces. Now she was the very grown up, utterly daunting first female pilot of the secretive Special Operations Aviation Regiment (airborne), flying the 160th's most lethal helicopter and earning some of the country's highest medals.

Em had stepped in and saved his life. He could think of no person he respected more. Nor any person who was a better judge of character, not even himself or Daniel. He had also never seen Em, who so rarely laughed, so light and easy as she was around Geneviève. They had chatted, teased, and joked like long-lost sisters, the shining blond and the dark French-Vietnamese beauty.

At the end of the evening, Em had pulled him aside. "We took a vote, oh pal of mine. She's great. So if you mess this up, we're all going to drop you and hang out with her. Don't blow it or you'll be answering to me. We clear?"

He was clear. He'd never been threatened by Beale over a woman before. Well, there was Mitsy in tenth grade, but that was a threat to hurt him if he didn't get rid of her.

Geneviève... He now so enjoyed saying her name and letting it roll off his tongue that he couldn't imagine using her nickname. Geneviève had changed the White House for him. He had loved the work, the challenges, the successes, even the failures. But living here had brought no joy. The first nine months, knowing that Katherine was sleeping just on the floor above scheming, had been something he'd done his best to ignore, but it had definitely not brightened his days. The two years since her death, he'd done little more in the Residence than sleep or attend state functions.

In a single night, Geneviève had filled the Residence with joy and laughter. Friends and family had come together and they had all enjoyed being together. It was only the second week of December, and it was already his best Christmas in recent memory, perhaps ever. Christmas at his parents had been quiet affairs, this had been noisy, ridiculous, fun, and filled with cookies. What more could a sane man ask for?

The dark beauty sleeping before him had won over more than the approval of his parents and friends. She had won his heart as well. It was not a familiar feeling, but it felt as if it should be. As if now for the first time, his own feelings were finally in the right place. Even though it was somewhere they had never been before.

He rose and undressed. Before he slipped into bed beside her, he spotted a cookie resting on the middle of his pillow. He groaned. Sugar still permeated the very air he was breathing and here was yet more. She must have slipped across the hall during the cookie making without his noticing and placed it here.

But it wasn't a Santa or any other shape they had made that night. It was a sugar-cookie heart, half white dough and half chocolate, baked almost as golden as Geneviève's skin. The two-colored dough had been merged not with a straight line, but in a swirl, as if they were inseparably wound together. Delicately decorated with a skilled hand that had outshone all of the rest of them as they iced their cookies. Geneviève had piped a simple outline in Christmas red.

Inside the perimeter of the heart, she had piped a simple message in green script: GB+PM.

Oh God.

She felt the same way about him as he did about her.

What were they going to do about that?

Chapter 8

As you may or may not know, and again this is not some secret stalking thing, I'm going to be in Southeast Asia for several days right before Christmas."

Genny focused on her luncheon omelet trying to decide if she was really awake yet. She'd slept right up to midday. By the time she had done her workout, showered, and entered the kitchen, it had been cleaned by the magical elves of the White House staff. Last night everyone had pitched in to clear and wash up the worst of the mess, but now it sparkled.

The mountainous stacks of cookie boxes were gone to the shelters, all down the tiny elevator in the corner of the kitchen. It connected the kitchens on the Second and Third Floors of the Residence with the big kitchen on the Ground Floor, and the Butler's Pantry on the First Floor used to organize and deliver state dinners. Even the boxes prepared for FedEx to go to Daniel's, Mark's, and Genny's families were gone.

Emily had left with a plateful for Mark and her parents consisting of broken cookies and design disasters, because she insisted none of them would care. And if they did, she didn't. They could just come and cook next year if they didn't like it.

Genny so admired the woman's strength, Emily's absolute centeredness in who she was. Genny wished she could do the same, but all she could manage was to study her omelet and not shudder at the huge changes rippling out of control across her life.

Peter had joined her for lunch. He'd left a note asking her to dial an extension when she was awake and ready to eat. When she called, she'd been connected, not to one of the President's secretaries as she'd expected, but rather directly to Peter in the Oval Office. She'd wager that few had such a privilege.

Lunching with the American President, sharing his bed, enjoying his friends. This was not a life she understood. Meetings with reluctant U.N. Ambassadors, fighting for proper patrols against poachers from understaffed park rangers who were probably on the take to look the other way, who had to be on the take to afford to feed their families. Those she understood.

"Who are you meeting with?"

"The Association of Southeast Asia Nations." He picked up his BLT sandwich and took a bite.

"Yes. Of course. I forgot all about the ASEAN meeting. The meeting is in Hanoi this year. Kicked out of Indonesia by yet another typhoon and disastrous flooding." Genny rubbed her eyes. She really wasn't awake yet.

That was a total fib, even to herself. She was wide awake and trying to figure out how to deny to herself what was happening between her and this man. She knew almost nothing about him, other than she was happy almost every minute they were together. For her, the existence of love at all was in question. At "first sight" was *très ridicule*. A myth. It had to be. But then why did she feel this way?

Okay, perhaps it wasn't at first sight. For six months she had watched every speech he'd made. And a pair of biographies were on her e-reader as well, ones that she'd actually gotten around to reading, unlike the latest Annie Ernaux novel, never mind all of the reports and studies she was inundated with daily.

She knew an immense amount about this man, even items that weren't in his biography, his passion for Scrabble among others. And that his best friend Emily Beale had merely been identified as a neighbor of his childhood in both biographies. Portions of his life were private.

So, even if it wasn't love at first sight, it was still going too fast.

"Yes. So, we'll be in Hanoi together." Genny ate some of the salmon omelet with English muffins that the main kitchen had sent up for her. The coffee was good, stronger than the last she'd had at the White House, even if it was served in monstrous American-sized cups. Not as good as home, but it helped.

"I'd like to see you when I'm there."

"No, Mr. President, you'd like to sleep with me while we are there and I would like that very much also."

Peter grinned, "Okay, caught me. That too. But I'd also like to meet your family while I'm there."

Genny went very still. She became aware of the weight of the fork in her hand, the scent of fresh basil still rising from her luncheon, and her heart stopped absolutely still in her chest.

"Why?"

He didn't even bother to answer. Instead, he left a silence as if to say, "This is so obvious we don't need to talk about it, but it is also still too new and uncomfortable for us to actually talk about it."

"Why?" She knew the answer. Why was she insisting on the words?

He set down his sandwich and sipped some ice tea as he considered his words.

"As President, I must often make fast decisions based on too little information. And I have to be right every time or the newspapers will shred me, publically, before I have a chance to correct it. My job is interpreting a thousand different factors, okay, maybe only hundreds, definitely dozens," his smile was easy. "As fast as I possibly can."

She nodded for him to continue, her head was the only part of her she was able to move. Her hand still suspended her fork halfway through slicing off the next bite of omelet.

"By contrast, in my personal life, I have with only one exception, always moved slowly and carefully. And that one exception led me to a dreadfully unhappy marriage."

There was another item not in the biographies. The country had worshipped and mourned Katherine Matthews. It was a topic of many articles and television shows right now because the President was seeing a foreign-national hussy who worked for the United Nations, who could never live up to the standards set by the amazing Katherine Matthews.

"I too do not want to be moving too fast. I do not want to do what I did to poor Gérard or suffer the many petty cruelties he did to me. You will need to be explaining about your wife to me."

Peter didn't look happy about that. He set down his sandwich as if it had lost all flavor for him.

"There are issues of national security here."

"There are issues of personal trust if we are to be in a relationship here." She managed to release her fork and folded her hands on the table before her.

Peter dragged a hand through his hair. "Can we just table this for later?"

"Mr. President," she didn't use the slight teasing tone that had become a part of her refusal to use his Christian name. She used the tone she might use addressing the U.N. General Secretary or any other head of state.

"Even if your relationship with your wife was a matter of national security, though I do not see how that is possible, there is a mutual trust that will be required or we will not be moving forward from this moment. We will not be sleeping together in Hanoi and you will not be meeting my family just as a contingency plan in case you happen to decide you want to propose to me at some later date. I trusted Gérard to be who he said he was, rather than who he turned out to be. I will not be making that mistake again."

Genny steeled herself to state the next line, but it must be said.

"Now," she kept her voice rock steady though her heart wanted to shatter inside her chest. "Do I stand up and go back to New York and you can tell your press briefing room that it was fun but didn't work out, which I will not gainsay? Or, do you explain why you are considering marriage with me when your first marriage was a public lie? Would ours be a lie as well?"

That she feared she might die inside if his answer was for her to leave, she did her best to ignore.

# # #

Peter rested his elbows on the kitchen island and buried his face in his hands just so he wouldn't have to look at Geneviève. How could she appear calm, waiting as patiently as Jonah crouched inside his whale?

His head was whirling so fast he couldn't begin to sort out the pieces. *Think, Peter. Just think!* It was an instruction he often shouted at himself when everything was spinning out of control in a political crisis situation. If he just thought his way through it, he could eventually find the starting point. The center that had caused the problem and escalated until the resulting problem was almost unrecognizable.

But he wasn't finding the starting point here. He knew she waited patiently, but that probably wouldn't last for long. She was an immensely practical woman and he was a damned mess. All he knew was that his world would crumble, that it would be far less happy, less bright, if she were to leave.

He looked up and faced her across their forgotten meal. This was not how he'd pictured their quiet luncheon together. A glance at the clock on the stove behind Geneviève told him he had about ten minutes to straighten this out before he was due back in the Oval Office. Ten minutes to figure out how to keep his love life heading wherever it was heading. Like that was going to happen. At least he could start. He knew one thing for sure.

"I don't want you to leave."

She sagged, "Thank God!"

He laughed aloud. He couldn't help himself. "You mean that you were sitting there so calm, beautiful, and perfect and scaring me half to death, and you were only doing it to make me crazy?"

"No, I am sitting here so worried, afraid, and such a mess, praying that you want to be with me."

"Christ, Geneviève. I didn't ask to meet your parents so that I could keep having sex with you."

She nodded, then nodded again as if registering that somewhere deep inside, and then went quiet again. She still wanted her answers.

Okay. So, she wasn't running away from him, as long as he didn't screw this up. He had a choice. While he might not trust a Vietnamese national, their relationship with the United States was still not the most comfortable, could he choose to trust this special woman? Trust that she would keep confidential that which had been so carefully kept secret.

Not trusting Geneviève felt like not trusting himself.

"Do you remember the video of that last flight? It was on all of the world media."

"Yes," she nodded. "A mechanical failure in the First Lady's helicopter, and the pilot was not good enough to save her life."

"I will offer you a different perspective. One that would not go well in the news."

Her look informed him he was being an idiot to doubt her discretion, which was probably true.

"What you may not recall is that Emily Beale was the pilot and only one person besides myself knows that her husband Mark was aboard as well."

"Well, that certainly takes pilot failure out of the picture. Wait!" Geneviève sat bolt upright as if she'd just been electrocuted. "You had them kill your wife?"

"No! No!" Now there was a conclusion he hadn't expected her to jump to. "Are Americans truly perceived as so cavalier by other countries? No, don't answer that, I don't want to get sidetracked. And besides, can you see Emily doing such a thing?"

"No," Geneviève shook her head and resettled. "No. Sorry. Tell your story."

"There are under ten people on the planet who know this next fact. Not even Daniel knows, though he suspects. Captain, now Major Emily Beale was shot during that flight."

He could see her mind working swiftly. It was only moments for her to absorb those facts and restructure the story herself before she spoke. By the look of sudden compassion and understanding in her eyes, he could see that she had realized that the only other person on that flight was Katherine Matthews. And that if someone had shot Major Beale, it had to be the First Lady who had pulled the trigger.

"Ah! I can't be sure of the timing, Mr. President, but it seems to me that approximately a month later you had a new White House Chief of Staff in Dr. Daniel Darlington. After your own Chief of Staff retired for health reasons?" She turned that into a question at the last moment. Then, "Your Chief of Staff didn't retire for health reasons. He was a part of it somehow."

Damn! He kept forgetting just how smart Geneviève was. Even Daniel couldn't put together apparently unrelated events as quickly. Yet another reason she swept Peter's feet out from under him.

"That's as long as we could delay the news. Ray Stevens did retire for 'health reasons,' so that he wouldn't be tried for treason as an unwitting pawn in the First Lady's plot. She planned to frame him for the murder of the President, and then to take over the country by marrying the bachelor Vice President, who she thought she was well on the way to controlling. Zach Taylor is a better man than that, though."

Peter wondered where she would go next, how many leaps would she make beyond the expected.

"Your taste in women apparently leaves something to be desired, Mr. President." She took up her fork and resumed eating as if the conversation were suddenly concluded.

"Until now."

"You're sweet." Her smile said much more.

"No, just enamored."

"Just enamored?"

"Deeply enamored?"

"You are so very male, Mr. President. But I will agree to that phrase. I too am deeply enamored. It is a good word."

"Only eleven points."

"Yes, but it uses all seven letters if played across a single letter, Mr. President. A nice bonus."

"A nice one indeed."

"So, how do we get you to my family plantation? It is not in Hanoi, but you will want to see it. And Gram, our matriarch, does not enjoy to travel often anymore. You should also get to see at least one World Heritage Site if you are to visit Southeast Asia."

Chapter 9

And by what method do you justify this to your American taxpayers?" Genny waved a hand to indicate herself seated aboard Air Force One, in the corner of the President's in-flight office. There had been only a few high-level meetings where she had retired to one of the equally comfortable seats in the corridor to afford him privacy. For the most part they both had sat quietly and worked. Now they were ten hours into the seventeen-hour flight and sharing a meal.

She was surprised to learn that dining on the President's airplane was nothing special. They served airplane fare, high quality and tasty, but she'd eaten far fancier menus when flying first class on Air France or SAS. Corned Beef on Rye along with potato salad, a fruit bowl, and a bag of chips. She drank a very nice wine and he a beer.

She didn't doubt that Peter would have a perfectly valid explanation of how he was not bilking the taxpayer in the slightest. She liked hearing such explanations from him, poking holes in them where she could. Which was always difficult because he was such an ethical man. Twice this week, he had brought a tricky problem from his workday to their bed and used her as a sounding board until he found a tenable solution.

Their bed. The President's bed. The lines were already blurring and she honestly didn't know how to feel about it. She decided that she wouldn't think about it until her family had a chance to meet

Peter and she could ask Gram's advice. Genny knew she was in over her head, but her Vietnamese grandmother was wise in many ways.

In the week between the cookie night and the flight to Hanoi, she had actually been able to work mostly from the White House, only spending two days in New York. Peter had set her up with an office in the Residence. She didn't need much, her laptop, phone, and a fax/copier on loan from the IT department had filled most of her needs.

Air Force One had actually afforded her some peace. By refusing to use the aircraft's telephone system, she'd been able to get a fair amount of work done, though she did appreciate her guest access to the on-board wireless network so that she could continue the never-ending battle with her e-mail.

"I just tell them," Peter saluted taxpayers everywhere with a tipping of his beer. "That I'm not going anywhere without my main squeeze along."

"Main squeeze?"

"Sorry, American slang. Old slang from my parents' youth, maybe even earlier. It means my main girl."

"And you have so many others that you are not telling me about? I maybe am part French which makes me understanding, but I am also part Vietnamese and that makes me possessive and dangerous."

Peter didn't even have the decency to squirm. "You're the main one for me."

"*Tu es impossible!*"

"And proud to be."

# # #

Despite Peter's hints about his private cabin and an opportunity to join the Mile-High Club, Genny had decided that wouldn't be a good idea with his staff so close by.

She had defused part of it by making him explain just what kind of club it was, as if she didn't know. He was far from the first man to proposition her in flight, though he might eventually be the first to succeed. So, she questioned him to evade the request, for now.

Did one only have to claim to have had sex over a mile in the air or was some form of proof required? And where did one register for this club of his? Did it count to have sex a hundred feet in the air over Denver, the Mile-High city? Were there extra points for higher altitudes? What about over each different country?

At least she had sent him to his rest with a laugh on his face and a kiss on his lips. But it had also left her at loose ends. She had worked some more, then watched part of a movie, but she was too *agité* from being on Air Force One to sleep. And, though she was reluctant to admit it, terribly nervous to be introducing Peter to her family.

Even one of the comfortable chairs reserved for senior staff didn't enable her to settle for more than a few pages into her latest novel. So she took herself on a tour of the plane. After all, if things went poorly in Vietnam, this might be her only chance.

The communications room in the 747's upper level was clearly off limits, the armed Air Force guard watching her expressionlessly from the top of the steps was an unnecessary emphasis on this point. Her interest in the galleys and storage on the lower deck was also minimal, and she had boarded through the forward galley, so she skipped the downward stairs just as she had the upward ones. Most people entered through the lower level, staff to the front and press to the rear.

Only the President and the occasional special guest entered the plane from the long rolling ramp to the middle deck hatch. He had wanted her to join him for the long climb up those stairs in front of all the cameras. She was tempted, but her nerves had won out. If this didn't work out between them, and she couldn't imagine how it possibly could in the long term, then she would forever be "That Girl" in the photo, boarding Air Force One to sleep with the President in flight.

Just outside the President's on-board office, Frank and Beatrice of the Secret Service sat together in the two reserved seats. Agent Belfour stood as soon as she spotted Genny.

"Everything okay, ma'am?"

"That's Genny to you, Beatrice. Or I will not answer when you speak to me."

"Right, sorry. That habit is going to die hard." She offered one of her bright smiles. "Anything I can do for you?"

"No. I am just touring the plane a bit. I'm tired of sitting and needed to move about."

"Yeah, these long flights are tough."

"I haven't been causing you trouble, have I?"

"Genny, you are a seriously easy charge. Besides, gives me a chance to travel with my husband which hasn't happened much over the years." Frank looked up at her. She hadn't had much to do with him, though he'd always been pleasant enough. For some reason it took Genny until this moment to realize that these were the two people from whom Peter was specifically not asking for background information about her.

Agents Frank Adams and Beatrice Belfour would know everything about her. From Genny's first boyfriend, a lovely young lad named Huang who would carry her books as he walked her home from secondary school, to her politics, pretty much didn't have those, couldn't afford them in her job. Well, if someone had to know all about her, she couldn't feel much more secure than these two. The Head of the Presidential Protection Detail and his wife were a force to be reckoned with.

Frank had a file open in his lap. She could see the photographs of the Preah Vihear temple, one of the possible World Cultural Heritage Site visits Genny had suggested. She'd specifically suggested that temple as it was in Cambodia, offering him a high profile visit that might help the U.N. with the site's preservation. It would also assist him with cultural relations with Cambodia by showing interest in their problems with their Thai neighbors. It was an area with some border issues that were still unresolved despite a hundred years of efforts at all levels, from the 1962 International Court of Justice ruling to her own minor efforts at the meeting where she had met the President last July.

Genny waved Beatrice back to her chair. "Well, you clearly have a lot of planning to do. I think that I will continue my tour. I suppose I can't get in too much trouble on an airplane."

"As long as don't try climbing the stairs, you're cleared for the entire plane." Beatrice tapped the badge with the letter "Q" dangling about Genny's neck.

She looked down at the badge in surprise. She hadn't really thought about it, though she hadn't seen another like it. A foreign national at liberty aboard Air Force One. Sitting in the President's on-board office as his assistants rushed in and out. It had felt normal, expected, not deeply unusual as it must be.

Beatrice nodded as if reading Genny's thoughts.

"Not only did the President insist, but you also checked out as alarmingly apolitical, discrete, and trustworthy among many other unseemly habits. That badge gets you anywhere in the Residence or on the grounds unescorted, into the West Wing with minimal escort, namely me, and Air Force One, except up those stairs."

"Oh, all right. Thanks." Beatrice returned to her seat and Genny took several steps away to peer into the next room. It was the medical room which included a doctor, a nurse, and a fold-down operating table that they were proud to tell her had never been used. Next, in their own small conference area, she nodded to three senior staff who she was beginning to recognize. Too bad Daniel wasn't along, though he'd probably be even busier than the President.

Again she looked down at the piece of plastic dangling about her neck. The red, white, and blue pattern and the letter "Q" which could have any number of meanings. Though, as the badges changed with each President, perhaps the "Q" badge was Peter's handiwork. Did it mean she had James Bond-style clearance all the way to "Q" the exotic weapons specialist? Or…

Then she had it. "Q" was a ten-point letter in Scrabble. It denoted that she was the highest value of visitor who still needed a badge. If Peter was involved there would be some meaning beyond the colors of the flag. Red for Residence, White for West Wing, and Blue for the color of Air Force One seemed likely. "RWB" would be worth eight points. With the Red being the color for Triple Word Score and Blue denoting Triple Letter Score, it would be worth, she calculated for a moment, forty-two points.

Genny decided that someone should put her out of her misery now. If she stayed with Peter much longer, she would become a complete mental case. Then she wondered. The badge had several layers of those shifting-background-image hologram effects, so that it would be very hard to duplicate. She held it up to a light and twisted it around for a moment. Sure enough, the deepest layer was a large "42." That did it. They should never be together. Two such nerds couldn't be allowed to exist in the same space.

With a sigh, she dropped the badge back to dangle about her neck and continue her tour. She really did like that man.

Genny wandered past the big conference and dining room without finding a soul to talk to. Most of the people in the staff and secretarial area were sleeping in their chairs, though one or two kept their eyes on the status of messaging to and from the aircraft. It was the dead of night in the middle of a seventeen-hour flight presently over the central Pacific, not much was going on.

She had half hoped to chat with the U.S. representative to ASEAN, but both he and his assistant were asleep in their guest seats. She was beginning to feel like the *Flying Dutchman,* forever haunting her ghostly ship. She had to reach the end of this aircraft at some point. It was only a little over two-hundred feet long, even if it felt like two-hundred meters.

Genny stepped through a doorway and discovered she had indeed reached the rear of the aircraft, and made a crucial mistake. Here at the rear were fourteen seats for the Press Corps. Most of the reporters were asleep, a few were eating a snack and watching a movie.

One woman, who Genny recognized as being from one of the networks, glanced up. For a moment her eyes spread so wide that it was hard to credit, then she recovered.

"Ms. Beauchamp." The woman's words galvanized the entire cabin into action. Fourteen people scrambled for cameras, recorders, even paper pads. They slapped seat neighbors to wake them up, pointing frantically toward Genny when they looked up in bewilderment.

She had avoided the press, carefully not saying a word whenever they mobbed her at the train station or airports. She had watched Peter on national television state, "Yes, we are seeing each other. But, no, I will not be reporting to you on any of the details beyond that. Ms. Beauchamp is my guest and I shall respect her privacy. She may speak for herself if she so chooses, but I have promised not to invade her privacy any more than I already have."

Well, perhaps now was her moment.

Looking out at the rows of faces, Genny nodded to the woman who had spotted her, granting her the first question. Knowing full well that all she had to do was take a step backward beyond the door if she wanted to get away.

# # #

When Peter had woken after a couple hours, more of a nap than he usually managed on these flights, he had to ask and wait while

Geneviève was tracked down as being with the reporters who rode in the rear of the plane.

He'd hustled down the length of the plane, Frank and Beat sweeping in behind him, but unable to overtake him. What had she been thinking?

"How long?" he barked back over his shoulder.

"Half an hour maybe," Beat replied. "I didn't think she'd go into the Press Corps area."

"Shit!"

Frank and Beat had the good sense not to correct his language. Each area went electric as he hurried through and he didn't give a damn. He ignored all questions, well aware of the consternation he was causing, and again couldn't care less. Frank reassured the other agents as they moved along.

Ten feet from the Press area, just at the head of the rear stairway, he stopped so abruptly that Frank actually ran into him, and had to grab his shoulders to keep from toppling him to the ground.

"Sorry, Mr. President."

He nodded, not trusting his voice. Taking a deep breath, he moved up to the cracked open edge of the doorway…and heard laughter. Geneviève's laughter, it was a sound he could pick out, even in the middle of a busy construction site. What had she… He listened without revealing himself.

"Yes," Geneviève was saying. "The French actually have this meal with three tablecloths and three white candles for the Father, Son, and the Holy Ghost. Seven dishes without meat for the seven sorrows of the Mother Mary, and thirteen desserts for the Apostles and Jesus. No matter what you believe, if eating thirteen desserts does not make you want to celebrate the life of such a man, then there must be something broken in you. Though my family is from Languedoc region, we are very smart and we take this Provençal tradition with us when we return to Vietnam. That is a proper holiday feast. Where you get this Roast Beef and Yorkshire Pudding, this I do not understand at all. Where is tradition in such a thing?"

"It tastes good," some reporter piped up.

"Okay," Geneviève replied merrily. "Yes, this I will grant. It tastes wonderful, but for Christmas in France or among the eight percent of Vietnam peoples who are Christians, it is not."

Peter moved through the door. The space was narrow, the rear of the plane had been cut into two sections. On the port side, it was an area for Secret Service and other flight security personnel. On the starboard side, were fourteen comfortable seats in pairs to either side of a narrow aisle. A lavatory on his right was the limit to how far the Press Corps were allowed to wander from their seats.

In the midst of the room, perched comfortably on the arm of a chair, sat Geneviève, looking as if she were entertaining casually in her own living room. Her thick hair pulled forward over one shoulder. The green turtleneck, just the shade of her eyes, hugged her amazing figure. Again that tiny silver Chinese character medallion was her only adornment. He couldn't imagine a more photogenic woman, and apparently neither could the Press Corps who appeared totally captivated.

Those nearest the entrance to the Press Cabin had their backs turned toward him, facing their guest. Those to the rear didn't notice his arrival.

She did though, the very second he entered. Just the briefest sidelong glance from those almond eyes, and a slight brightening of her smile.

"Well, it has been a pleasure to meet you all."

The sounds of disappointment that washed around the room sounded deeply genuine.

Then her smile turned wicked and she carefully didn't look at him. "I did tell you that I would answer no questions about the President and me. That it was because, how would you like to have your fellow reporters and their news cameras in your bedroom?"

One of them actually shuddered theatrically eliciting a laugh from the others, as relaxed as Peter had ever seen the White House Press Corps.

"But perhaps I could tell you something, how do you say, off your record?"

They were so enamored of Geneviève, that they didn't even bother to correct her.

"You must promise."

They raised hands. Some as if swearing in on a Bible, a couple of boy scout and girl scout salutes, a Vulcan hand sign, and two traditionalists with a hand over their heart. He knew as President of the United States never to trust the Press Corps, but he'd half wager they'd keep a secret for foreign national Ms. Geneviève Beauchamp.

"Good. I will tell you one thing that I have learned. Your President Matthews has never made love to a woman in the Oval Office of the White House. He is afraid, as if he would be first in your history to do so."

Then she looked right at him. The reporters followed her gaze and then startled to find the President standing in their company.

"I think," Geneviève's eyes were positively sparkling as she spoke loudly enough to be heard over the bustle of everyone turning to face him. "I think we need to convince him it could be fun." Her smile, now for him alone as all of the reporters were turned in his direction, acknowledged that it would scare the daylights out of both of them to make love right in the center of that bloody carpet with the portraits of the past Presidents looking on.

Peter did his damnedest not to blush as they all looked at him with knowing smiles.

He was sure he didn't succeed.

Chapter 10

*A*re *we really sure* this is the best option?" Peter looked at the itinerary Frank had worked up. They sat at Noi Bai Airport in his office aboard Air Force One after the second long day of ASEAN meetings. He had slept aboard, as it had offered him the best secure communications as well as being highly defensible. Geneviève had stayed in the city until now, far busier than even he was, and he had missed her terribly.

"There are two ways to approach this, sir. We can let everyone know the President is arriving at an old French plantation in the Northern Highlands of Vietnam far too close to the Laotian border for my taste. We can do this after taking three to six months to plan, then insert heavy U.S. and Vietnamese forces to lock down the entire area."

Peter looked at Geneviève who merely shrugged. Clearly the woman had enough sense to know when she was out of her depth, but so was he.

"The second option," Frank continued, "is to mimic the flight you made last year to Nevada with Majors Beale and Henderson. Simply don't let anyone know you're there and move with a minimal force. To this end, we have taken advantage of an offer from Vietnam's Prime Minister. He is quite pleased that Ms. Beauchamp, a Vietnamese national, is 'your guide' for this trip to visit one of their most successful farming collectives and only regrets that he will be unable to join you himself."

Frank glanced at Geneviève, but his expression was unreadable. Perhaps he worried that the Prime Minister's careful word choice would offend her. Then Frank continued.

"The moment you authorize this, a body double will climb aboard the Marine One helicopter we brought from the States and will fly him to a quiet evening at the Prime Minister's personal residence. Ten minutes later, you will climb aboard Major Beale's chopper, presently in the country on a training and good will exercise, and we will proceed to the Beauchamp plantation with a minimal guard force."

Peter knew he was unqualified to make the final decision on this one, he was far too biased in favor of going.

"What do you think, Frank?"

# # #

It took twenty minutes, rather than ten, before Peter was clambering aboard a Black Hawk helicopter of the 160th SOAR. He wore a standard flightsuit and survival vest as did Geneviève and their two Secret Service agents. They blended in easily among the busy goings-on at the area of Noi Bai airport that had been reserved for the use of the visiting Americans.

The two Black Hawks were transport versions, but still had the two mini-guns manned. A half-dozen Secret Service agents piled into one. Frank guided Peter to the second one. Four seats had been arranged in the low-ceilinged cargo bay. His and Geneviève's facing forward, Frank and Beat sitting backward to face them. The two crew chiefs made sure they were buckled in. They were small, even for Special Forces. They had their helmets on and visors down, but he'd bet these were Sergeants Connie Davis and Kee Smith. This was Beale's elite crew. He felt safer already.

They were barely buckled in before they were aloft. They had left the large cargo bay doors open, which was good. Even though evening was approaching, it was ninety degrees and about a thousand percent humidity. He'd been assured that even locals were wilting beneath the unusually warm weather for this time of year.

"Welcome aboard, Army One, sir." Mark Henderson greeted him as soon as he pulled on a headset. It was the proper call sign for an Army helicopter carrying the President. Though it certainly wouldn't be announced to any Vietnamese flight controllers. "This evening we will be simulating a training flight to the mountains west of Vinh, Vietnam. We anticipate a quiet flight with the cooperation of General Chu Huang who created a no-fly corridor for this exercise. He did ask us to provide a special greeting to Ms. Beauchamp."

Peter glanced over at Geneviève, who merely smiled at him. A glance at Frank and Beat revealed they recognized the name.

"Okay, give."

Geneviève shrugged, "He was a cute boy. He used to carry my books in secondary school. But then he left me before third year for another woman. I was heartbroken."

"Why would any sane man ever leave you?"

"You have never met Lê Mei, Mr. President. I must make sure you do not. She was so very beautiful. They are married and have a boy and girl, I believe."

He tried to imagine someone more beautiful than the woman beside him, but could think of no examples. Then he caught the wistful tone of Geneviève's voice as she spoke of the children. He didn't know how he felt about that. With he and Katherine there had never been any question. Even when they were still sharing the same bed and he had thought they were happy, it was clear that she would never slow down enough to have children.

With Geneviève… It was not something they had spoken of, but he could imagine her with children. How would she continue her work, though? How would she do that if she stayed with him? The topic was becoming much too complicated, so he kept his mouth shut and put the thoughts aside to admire the view out the open cargo bay door. It was really too hot and humid to close it.

They climbed out of Hanoi, circling to the west. Vietnam was a sunrise country. All of its coastline, except a small area far to the south, faced the Pacific Ocean to the east. The sun rose from the water and set beyond high mountains. They were out of the city quickly. Even the suburbs surrounding a city of six million faded away soon into lush farmlands.

"I didn't realize there was so much wetlands."

"We are over the Red River Delta, a vast and very fertile region, Mr. President," Geneviève pointed toward the ocean. "The coast is eighty kilometers away, yet Hanoi is only twenty-one meters above sea level, seventy feet. You really must do something about that. Do you know that only your country, Liberia, and Myanmar still use those English units? Even England has mostly changed over to metric."

"I'll make a note of that." He admitted that it was ridiculous, but knew it was a battle not worth fighting. Perhaps in his second term when tilting at impossible windmills was considered eccentrically permissible for the Commander in Chief. He looked down upon miles of lakes, rivers, and streams and fields. "There must be tens of thousands of bridges."

"More, I am sure, though I have never counted."

As the farmland decreased, the lush vegetation increased, soon the jungle was underlain by sharp ridges like none he had ever seen. As if the countryside was an entire mountain range, the valleys of which had been filled in by millions of years of silt. That, he speculated, was exactly what had happened. It made for a strange mix in his head. *Homo sapiens* had arrived here half-a-million years before crossing over to the Americas fifteen-thousand years ago. Yet, in sharp contrast, the land had a vitality, a life that sprang forth and covered the country.

The contrast of old and new should not have been surprising, but it was to him. Europe felt old and well contained, all so carefully groomed. Africa was ancient and weary, lost in arid wastelands and wild jungles. Here there was the vitality of a country constantly rediscovering itself, building itself anew, undaunted by past wars or more history than he could imagine.

The chopper climbed up river valleys and over ridges.

"My family lives very close to Pu Mat National Park, which is the edge of the Highlands. We are at a hundred meters, though parts of the park are over a thousand. It was a rubber plantation that my ancestors started in the 1920s. When we returned after the Vietnam War, we converted it to coffee. It was a very large holding. One of the few that the North Vietnamese government was glad to preserve intact because of how well my family had managed it. We were welcomed back most kindly. We now own it as a cooperative in partnership with the state and the workers, and it is functioning very well. For example, Vietnam has a ninety percent literacy rate, better in the city, worse in the country. We pay for all of our workers' schooling. My family has always done that, so now we have close to one hundred percent literacy among even our oldest workers."

Peter looked down at the terrain. A wide river meandered through the low mountains. As they descended toward a large villa surrounded by tall trees, Peter could see the coffee. Hundreds of acres, perhaps thousands were covered in long rows of man-high bushes. A wide diversity of shade trees to decrease erosion dotted the hillsides like punctuation marks. Unlike the vineyards of France that climbed vertically up the slope, these swooped around the terrain like a living topographic map, vast level fields suddenly bursting upward as hills bedecked in horizontal wreaths of deep-green plants over red soil. He breathed in, half expecting a rich coffee aroma, instead tasting the thickness of the air so full of growing plants.

It was so beautiful, foreign yet familiar in some way, as if Geneviève had already biased him toward her country. She had biased him toward many things he had not expected even a few weeks before.

# # #

Peter stepped off the second chopper into another world. They had landed in the front yard of the main plantation house. Tall, proud trees, that bore no resemblance to anything he was familiar with in the states, shaded the old plantation house. Even in the last light of day, he could see the mix of Western sturdiness in its two-story façade, squared windows and clapboard sides, enhanced with Asian details of ornate railings on the full-length porch, curlicues of the archway above the main entrance, and swooping lines to the roof. The siding shone a cheerful yellow. The roof was of dark, weather-worn wood shingle. What must have been a magnificent building a hundred years before had aged and grown stately rather than decayed.

He also couldn't help but notice the immense quiet as he dragged off his vest and flight suit. At first he'd thought it was merely because his ears had become conditioned to the helicopter's penetrating noise, despite the heavy headset. But as he listened, it was truly quiet. There were no cars, no busy Washington streets. Even Camp David, with its heavy patrols of Secret Service agents, was never so quiet.

"What are you listening to?" Geneviève came up beside him, but didn't take his hand.

"The sounds of your home." A late-nesting bird called in the evening light. Some distance off, he might have heard a horse whinny. "I'm not used to the quiet."

"It is something I forget about. I only miss it when I come home."

Despite their noisy arrival, and the sweep of Frank's team, no one came from the house to greet them.

"Maybe we scared off your family. I am a pretty scary guy after all."

"Nothing could scare off my family, Mr. President. They wait for you to enter as family, rather than to wait at the threshold as they would for a guest. Come, we keep them waiting and I'm sure they are shaking with excitement."

Peter was trying his best not to shake with nerves. It was ridiculous, but meeting Geneviève's family was turning into a far bigger fear than he had anticipated. Now he could appreciate some of her anger when his parents had simply dropped in. Though, he could almost wish for a similar experience himself, in over your head and then done with it. He'd had over a week for this to build in importance in his mind until it was a near to overwhelming tidal wave.

Beale and Mark and the others would be staying with the choppers to help provide security, so no help there. He was on his own this time. Mostly on his own. He had told the dozen agents and the SOAR assets that they could secure the outside, but that he would trust to the residents of the house himself.

He took Geneviève's hand in his. Her slight resistance told him that would not be appropriate, but she would hold his hand if he needed her to. He placed her hand in the crook of his elbow, just as he had that first night at the National Christmas Tree, took up the gift he had brought, and they turned for the house.

As they walked to the house and climbed the dozen front steps, she told him some of her family's history so that he would have something to think about while he was panicking.

"My mother, Adele, was five when my family was driven out of the country at the end of the French War and they returned to France. She grew up there with her father who could not remain in the North Vietnam of 1960, as he was pure French blood and they were killing all of the French at that time. He did return at the height of the American War. My mother was eighteen and gone to college. He spent five more years with my grandmother, but did not survive the purges that came after the war. So I never met him."

She stopped two steps from the top to give him a moment and kept telling her story. He could kiss her for her thoughtfulness. He really had to remember how to breathe.

"My mother returned at twenty-five with my father, Henri, on her arm. They had me when they were thirty. She and dad are very French, though they have been in Vietnam for almost forty years. Gram stayed here through the war. Even though she is a hundred percent Viet, we do not know how she survived the purges, but she did."

They set off again and reached the top step. The wide porch sported many chairs from a variety of lineages, clearly a common gathering space. A waist-high stone Buddha greeted him at the head of the stairs.

"I thought your family was French Catholic?"

Geneviève shrugged. "Just because we are Catholic does not mean we can't also revere Buddha."

Peter was just taking a breath preparatory to knocking, when Genny threw open the door, leading him inside and called out, "We're home."

She was, but he was totally lost.

# # #

"These are my parents, Henri and Adele." They traded cheek-to-cheek kisses and then quick hugs with her. They then each greeted Peter similarly, though without the hugs.

Geneviève had her mother's hair and fine features, and her father's length, that was easy to see.

"These are my sisters. They are both pills." A pair of brunettes came forward. They showed none of their Vietnamese heritage. Both would have been taken as French natives, fair-skinned and round-eyed.

"I'm Helaine. That is Dr. Ngô Helaine, M.D." Her English was American and reflected little of her native languages. "UCLA and University of Washington. And she only hates us because we are better than her. I work at the main hospital in Vinh. A hundred kilometers toward the coast. My husband, a doctor too, is in surgery. He sends greetings as he is unable to attend." Her handshake was Western as well.

The second sister subtly hip-checked Helaine out of the way. "I'm Jacqueline and Helly is wrong." Her voice was higher, making her sound like a Valley Girl with a pronounced French accent. She was also the most curved of the three sisters and had cheerfully curly hair and a tight blouse that revealed a fair expanse of cleavage.

"Gen-Gen hates Helly because when she arrived, it ruined Gen-Gen's chance at being an only daughter. Gen-Gen hates me cause I got all the curves and she didn't. You're cute." She made a show of actually kissing Peter much to his surprise.

Then she winked to show she was just teasing her big sister.

"You should stay. I'm a doctor too you know. Business economics from the Sorbonne and Vietnam National University." Well, that belied the airhead image she projected. "We need another man here so that daddy can retire. How would you like to marry into the family business?"

She started to move in again, but thankfully Geneviève just shoved her aside with little ceremony. In revenge, Jacqueline stuck her tongue out at her big sister. Henri trapped his youngest daughter in a friendly headlock to forestall further rounds between the siblings.

Peter didn't know what to expect of Gram Kim-Ly Beauchamp, but it was certainly not the woman who strode up as if parting the Red Sea that was her family. Geneviève had said she would be eighty soon but she certainly didn't walk that way. The trim woman barely came up to his shoulder, but it wasn't because she was stooped. She appeared strong, almost athletic, apparently just arriving back home from a day in the fields managing the coffee crop.

A black dog stood at her side, stout, strong, and not friendly looking. That must be Dais, which meant Bear in the Hmong language. Geneviève had described him as sweet, gentle, and a stone-cold killer when needed, though primarily of unwanted rodents. Wonderful. That made him feel so much better.

The woman who clearly ruled the dog wore sturdy boots that were well used, gray khakis, and a white men's dress shirt with long sleeves rolled up to her elbows. Her gray hair hung straight and long. Here was Geneviève's stunning face and amazing green eyes aged, mellowed, and grown wise with time. Beauty, while it had touched on the other three women in the family, had mostly skipped a generation to land squarely on this woman's eldest granddaughter.

If not for the decades between them, Gram and Geneviève could be twins in all but height and the brush stroke of Adele's finer features.

"So, this is your President boyfriend." She folded her arms and bowed her head slightly to him. Her English was lightly French-accented.

"I am Ms. Beauchamp. I'm pleased to meet you." He did the same obeisance in return.

She stared up at him for a long moment. The room went silent. Even the dog stood still.

Peter half wondered if Geneviève was holding her breath. He would wager that she was. That's when he realized he was as well. Then he huffed it out and laughed before he turned to Geneviève.

"You're right. Your grandmother is deeply scary."

The others in the room laughed as well in understanding ways, though Gram's expression changed not even a little.

"And it is a trait," he turned to address the matriarch again in a more serious tone, "that you have very successfully passed on to your namesake."

Still the woman looked at him. Then she spoke to the dog, "Dais. Zaum."

The dog, who had been standing at alert and worrying Peter some fair amount, dropped to his haunches and his tongue had lolled out. He shifted from looking like a knee-high, angry, and dangerous bear, to a knee-high, not angry but could attack in a second, working dog.

"I think, young man, that you should call me Kim-Ly."

Geneviève's hand, somehow once again in the crook of his elbow, which had been clamping down painfully hard, abruptly relaxed, then squeezed again for a moment in reassurance.

"In that case, Kim-Ly, you must call me Peter. Especially as your granddaughter will not."

# # #

The meal had been long, and wholly untraditional. Mother had set the formal dining room, but Gram had vetoed that, declaring Peter as family, and they had moved to the big rough table in the kitchen. Genny had to fight back the tears. That Gram would so approve of him on first meeting meant that Genny was not going crazy. Of course, it meant… She really was not going to survive this day. She'd been able to feel Peter's nerves, but been able to do little to help him as she'd been in an absolute state of panic since the instant he had suggested coming here. Throughout the evening, Genny had been on the edge of cheering, laughing, or weeping. Or perhaps all three at once.

It had taken mere minutes from their arrival until it was as if Peter had sat a thousand times at the family table. And Genny's emotions were all over the map about that as well throughout the meal.

At least the order of the dishes made sense for a change. Normally at the Beauchamp table, there was no predicting what would be done and served first. They began with Jacqui's Vietnamese spring rolls, wrapped in nearly translucent rice dough. They had beef *Pho* followed by Gram's notorious Chicken Curry on Rice Noodles. It had left Peter so bright red and sweating so profusely that she hoped he didn't have a heart attack from the spicing.

It was perhaps the best meal Genny had ever barely tasted, all the familiar flavors of home. Every joke that came even close to her relationship with the President made her twitch. She couldn't remember from the beginning of one sentence to the end of it, what the subject might be.

Some remote part of her observed, *So, this is what an American means when they say they are totally freaked out. How interesting. I am indeed totally freaked out.* And that simple statement of fact about her emotions, well, it was freaking her out.

Jacqi swore that she'd made *Bánh phu thê*. Genny had searched the kitchen high and low for the South Vietnamese traditional "Husband and Wife" cakes so that she could throw them down the back steps. Instead, Jacqi had actually made Genny's favorite, *Bánh rán,* deep-fried sesame rice balls. They should have been an awful combination when served beside Peter's gift of American maple syrup-flavored fudge. But somehow, when combined with enough laughter and a fresh pot of decaffeinated coffee, they had tasted wonderful together.

Peter couldn't say enough praise for the coffee. At first everyone had assumed he was just being nice, but she knew better. She could tell when he was being disingenuous, and this was not one of those times. His sincerity became unmistakable when he began taking a real interest in their issues with exporting to the Americas. He begged them for at least a periodic care package that he would hoard in his own kitchen.

As the evening progressed, Genny wondered how to get her grandmother aside. Even after the meal, no one wanted to leave the table. There was a warmth, a friendliness that pervaded the room.

Genny passed through desperate and panicked on her way to resigned. She would just have to let go. Perhaps a phone call would be best, later in the week, or maybe next year. No, that was only two weeks away. Maybe the year after that. Though she had wanted to feel her grandmother's touch and see her as they spoke, but there was clearly no time for that to happen tonight.

So, Genny listened as Peter told the story of their first attempt to cook together which set off the smoke alarm in the Residence kitchen. He'd burned the French toast and she in turn had scorched the hot chocolate so badly they'd had to throw out the pot.

"Now," Gram announced as she rose to her feet at the end of Peter's story. "I must talk with my granddaughter. And then you, Mr. Peter President, must return to your plane before you are missed. Come, Genny." Gram turned for the door and, that simply, it was accomplished. Genny shuffled after her, feeling as if she were about twelve and was soon to be scolded.

# # #

Genny caught up with her grandmother exactly where she'd expected. Gram stood before the Weeping Wall in what had originally been the plantation's front parlor. Though connected to the family living room by a curved arch, it was wholly different in character. Favorite chairs and stacks of books and board games gave way here to a state-of-the-art office. The cooperative was managed from here, workers and their families welcomed right into the main house if they needed anything.

Now, in the light of a single lamp, all of that was but shadows. Desks, phones, copiers, computers, none of that mattered. What mattered was the powerful woman and the wall covered with hundreds of photos, each memory preserved in a small wooden frame.

Genny came up beside the Beauchamp matriarch, wrapped her arm around the old woman's waist, and rested her cheek upon the gray hair. For a long time they stood and looked at the pictures. Generations of images adorned the wall.

She and her sisters growing up in pink pinafores and in traditional *áo dài* white dresses with circular *nón lá* leaf hats. Working on the farm together. Three pre-teen girls going off to school together, each two years apart. Even at that age, she had been the tall, gawky one, Jacqi rounder and smiling mischievously, and Helaine the serious one constantly trapped between them. There were dozens of photos of the three of them together through the years.

There were also photos of her sisters graduating, Helly working in a hospital operating room, Jacqi at her first computer. Helly with her half-Viet, half-Lao husband. Jacqi with many different boys.

And photos of Genny. Some she knew, some she didn't. A series of her wearing her blue *vophuc* fighting uniform and a progression of belt colors. As the colors changed, so did she, from a young girl to a woman grown. But there were also photos of her at World Heritage Sites talking to reporters, and even one of her arguing a case to the U.N. Security Council just a few weeks ago, a grainy shot that must have been captured from an Internet news site.

Her mother and father were there as well. Henri typically in the office with Jacqi looking over his shoulder, or more recently working beside him. Adele dressed like Gram, the two of them working the cooperative and a succession of Hmong dock-tail dogs accompanying them into the fields.

Uncles who had died during the purges were here, as well as Aunts who had died while fighting in the American War. And in the French War before that. And even her great, great granddad who had fought the guerilla war against the Japanese.

Gram and Grand were there too, mostly working the plantation before the war. There were pictures of them at their two weddings: one Catholic, one traditional Vietnamese.

"You looked so beautiful, Gram." The photo was black and white, but that did nothing to hide the rich splendor of her robe or the perfect shape of the circular *khan dong* rising from her hair like a crown of gold.

"As you will at your wedding, my dear," Gram spoke in Viet.

Genny looked at the Weeping Wall. At the wall that could make you weep for the pain of what was lost and at the same time for the wonder of what was gained. The wall always made her feel so full inside. As if, knowing where she came from, she could do anything.

"Right there," Gram pointed at a blank section of wall. "That's where I will put the photo of the day you marry the man you love."

Genny turned to look at her, as much as their arms around each others' waists allowed.

"But, how will I know, grandmother? I don't understand that."

"It's simple, child. You already know. It will just take you a little more time to find out that you know. But you will get there. And soon I will put up the photo."

Genny once more rested her cheek against her grandmother's hair and breathed in her rich smell of the farm life she still led. Of coffee and fan-palm, of jungle and river. Of home.

She studied the blank spot on the wall that Gram had chosen for her. Genny did not need to close her eyes to see the image that would hang there.

Her grandmother was right.

Genny already knew.

# # #

They spoke little on the flight back. The night and the helicopter were dark. Peter sat with his arm around Geneviève, holding her as close as he could without crushing her to him. And, as well as the headset allowed, she rested her head on his shoulder.

"Your family is wonderful," Peter had set them to have a private intercom but they had been mostly content with the silence. "Though I feel a touch of pity for whatever man Jacqi finally decides on."

"We all do. But for all that, she is an alarmingly sensible woman. The cooperative will continue very well under her management for many years. She loves the business, even more than mother. Maybe as much as Gram, if that were possible. I often think it is the only thing that grounds Jacqi on this planet."

More miles passed in silence. Peter was trying to assimilate Geneviève's family, to see them for who they were, rather than for the whirlwind that had just filled the last few hours of his life. Like digesting the gigantic meal they had prepared that still left his appetite feeling deeply content, he knew it was not something that could happen quickly.

"Your grandmother is everything you said and more."

Geneviève nodded her head against his shoulder.

"What did she say to you?"

Geneviève shook her head this time. She had been very quiet after her talk with her grandmother. Deep in thought. Not remote, just quiet.

"You are so like her."

"I am?" That brought her jolting upright so abruptly that her headset caught his chin and he bit his tongue hard.

"Ow! Yes."

"No, Jacqi is—"

"Like your father mixed with a California surfer girl right out of a Beach Boys song. Helaine has your mother's serious streak, those are two very formidable women. I still can't believe your mother came back while the re-education camps and long marches from the cities back to the country were still going on."

"But I'm not like Gram. She's—"

"Exactly like you. There is a peace and a centeredness to your strengths that runs so deep and so wide that you two are the great rivers others flow into. How's that for an appropriate metaphor while flying over the Red River Delta?"

They were approaching southern Hanoi now. By the city lights that washed into the night sky, he could see Geneviève staring at him. But not at him. It was as if she were staring at a reflection of herself in his face that she had never seen before. He found it so obvious that he wondered how she could not have known.

They swung around the western edge of the city on the last leg of their flight back to Noi Bai airport. The broad river was a dark anchor to the bright lights of the scattered skyscrapers and the busy city at their feet.

These were his last moments of being Peter. He could feel the Presidency lurking on the ground below him, waiting there like a crouched beast. Or like a mantle that, once pulled back over his shoulders, would change him. Change who he had been these last few hours with Geneviève and her family.

"There's something I need to say, Geneviève. Something while we are still in the air and I am not back to being the Commander-in-Chief."

She looked at him. Her focus changing from the reflection of herself back to that peaceful waiting she created so effortlessly for him.

This shouldn't be said over headsets and an intercom. But neither did he want to take them off and have to shout to her either, only to have her cup an ear and shout back, "What?"

But they were on final descent, and he had to speak while he still felt like Peter. He kissed her lightly on the lips, her widening eyes catching the airport lights and revealing their rich green as she guessed.

Did she hope, or fear? Well, there was only one way to find out.

"I love you, Geneviève."

Her kiss and the taste of her tears were the only answer he needed.

Chapter 11

Preah Vihear Temple was located at the northernmost edge of Cambodia, close to Thailand. It was over an hour-long helicopter flight from where Air Force One was parked at Phnom Penh International. They could have parked much closer, Siem Reap airport by Angkor Wat was within thirty minutes flight. The shorter runway would limit the take-off weight of the plane, but that could be compensated for with partial fueling. However, Peter had deemed it more politically appropriate for them to land in the capital city.

There he'd had lunch with both the King and the Prime Minister as well as key members of the Cambodian Parliament. Then, with their U.N. Ambassador and Deputy Prime Minister aboard, they had flown north on Marine One.

This trip was vastly different from the flight to Geneviève's, this was a full-on Marine Corps operation. Two VH-60N White Hawks, heavily armored versions of the Sikorsky Black Hawks, were the main flight. They jostled about, exchanging places in a shell game until no one except the pilots and their passengers knew which craft was which.

The Royal Cambodian Air Force provided a pair of their Aero L-39 Albatross ground attack jets to fly escort, and flight controllers had cleared a corridor twenty kilometers wide. Frank's briefing had selected this site, from the several Geneviève had suggested, as being the lowest-risk and most defensible for a Presidential visit. It had also been Geneviève's preferred location for cultural and political reasons.

"So, Ms. Beauchamp," Peter thought it best to keep it formal in front of the other officials, though any idiot would be able to see they were hopelessly crazy about each other. "Could you bring us up to speed on this site and UNESCO's involvement in it?"

Peter sat as he usually did in the White Hawk, in the sole, forward-facing armchair. Directly across from him, the Cambodian Deputy Prime Minister sat in the other armchair facing the back of the chopper. The small couch running along the other side of the cabin included the Cambodian Ambassador to the U.N., the U.S. Assistant Representative to ASEAN, and Geneviève, as the Southeast Asia Chief of Unit for UNESCO World Heritage Convention.

He had to keep reminding himself of that. She was so close, her knees practically brushing the side of his seat. She wore a skirt that came to just her knees. It was snug, but elegant. So easy to rest his hand on her knee, which would be unfair to her position of status among the others.

Frank sat in his typical spot, in the jump seat directly behind Peter's armchair. This chopper, unlike Emily's SOAR craft, was well enough sound insulated for them to talk without headsets.

"Well," Geneviève leaned forward, exposing the line of her neck.

Peter considered slapping himself, but knew it wouldn't help. There hadn't been a moment for them to discuss how she could possibly continue her career and be with the President of the United States. But it didn't matter. That she wanted to was all the answer that mattered at the moment. They had agreed not to tell anyone, neither staff nor family, until this trip was over. That would be only three more days. By then they should have figured out what to say to everyone.

"The temple is over a thousand years old, a masterpiece of the Khmer Empire, as is Angkor Wat, their capital city." She spoke easily, her voice engaging. "It is perched on a narrow promontory of the Dângrêk Mountains. This has caused both Cambodia and Thailand severe problems over the last century. The escarpment that separates the mountains from the Cambodian plains over five hundred meters below, was to be the line of the border. More correctly, the line of the watershed was to be the border. There were maps drawn in 1907, placing the temple and one of the approaches to it in Cambodia and another approach in Thailand. But the watershed line, had it been followed, would have placed all of the approaches in Thailand and only the temple itself in Cambodia. In 1962 the International Court of Justice became involved and ruled that because Thailand had not protested the border as drawn for almost sixty years, the 1907 map was valid and would stand."

Deputy Prime Minister Pok made an emphatic nod.

Peter had to force himself to remain focused on his guests. Geneviève had warned him that they would be entering a murky and emotional area when they discussed the border. But a fresh coup in two different African countries had cost him most of last night between the dinner with Geneviève's family and this flight. He'd crashed into his cabin for only two hours, pleased to see Geneviève asleep on one of the twin beds when he did so. She hadn't woken when he kissed her on the forehead, and she'd been awake and gone by the time he crawled back into his office.

"Yes," Pok insisted, nodding again as if it would make his statement more real. "It is the property of the Kingdom of Cambodia, just as is Angkor Wat. The Khmer Empire became Cambodia and it is rightfully ours."

The Cambodian Ambassador to the U.N., Moul, or was he Muy, looked apologetic. He thought it was Moul, but Peter would just have to be careful not to say his name until someone else did.

"I would not contradict the esteemed Minister Pok." Meaning the man had his facts totally wrong. "Suffice to say, the temple is on Cambodian soil, despite being atop the escarpment. Despite numerous international mandates and agreements, the Thai government places border stations and police barricades on these roads. They often close the road that is our only access to a piece of our own country. At other times, we have free passage."

"Yes," Geneviève stepped in before Pok, who was clearly getting ready to build a righteous national-pride argument, could begin. "Preah Vihear, a UNESCO World Heritage Site since 2008, represents both significant cultural pride as well as substantial tourist dollars. And the argument over this balance is beyond the purview of today's discussions, Mr. President." But she addressed the last to Pok, clearly a reminder of exactly who was important in today's visit.

"UNESCO is attempting to work with both governments to set up a free economic zone that is shared by both countries. The International Court has required both Thailand and Cambodia to withdraw their troops from the area. The two governments agree only that they can't withdraw unless the other does so first."

"It is Cambodian land, why should we move first?" Pok felt that completed his argument.

"We're flying into the heart of a military stand-off?" Peter glanced back at Frank not giving a damn if the officials heard. Better if they did, it would emphasize that the President of America felt they needed to get their act together.

Frank's deep voice carried forward easily. "Last shots were fired in February 2011. Forces remain in the area, but there have been no more hostilities since that time. Both Cambodian and Thai commanders have assured us that we will have a peaceful visit. They each separately stated that it was to our advantage to have so much military security in such an unusually remote locale."

"It is further suggested," Geneviève picked up without missing a beat "By the UNESCO Director, ASEAN Director, and concurred with by the U.S. State Department, that a site visit will demonstrate international commitment to a peaceful solution."

It was almost as if she and Frank had rehearsed the handoff from security to veiled threat of U.S. and U.N. military involvement. Peter glanced at Geneviève's carefully neutral expression. He'd learned to read that face over these last weeks. Yes, she had clearly planned that last speech which had Minister Pok squirming in his seat. He had to remember not to mess with her.

"We're approaching the site. We have been cleared to land at the end of the temple grounds, as the most readily securable location," the Marine Corps pilot announced.

Peter looked out the window. He tapped the intercom. "Could you circle once please?"

The pilot swung wide, keeping Peter's window toward the view. The flat plains of Cambodia which had climbed just a few hundred feet in the three hundred miles from the coast were chopped off by the Dângrêk Mountain escarpment. The Preah Vihear Temple itself was perched on a narrow promontory that reached half a mile into the plains compared with the rest of the rise.

"How—" He cut himself off before he could continue. It made no sense. The temple was atop the escarpment, the rest of which was Thailand. How this little piece had been snipped off and given to Cambodia must have a background story. But it would be very impolitic of him to call the Cambodian claim illogical, especially sitting with the country's Deputy Prime Minister and U.N. Ambassador.

But Geneviève had read his question anyway. "The original agreed border was the watershed. If it drained north, it was Thai. The temple grounds drain south. Then a line was drawn on a map a hundred years ago by people who had never been here and much of the north-draining land, including the crucial access road, were given to Cambodia. Now, it is a part of the area's history. Would you, Mr. President, be willing to give up Point Roberts?"

"Point Roberts?"

"In your Washington State. It is a tiny piece of British Columbia land that sticks into the middle of the Straits of Georgia. This piece of Canadian peninsula is technically United States soil because a line of the forty-ninth parallel was drawn as a border between your country and Canada in 1846. Would you be willing to give that up?"

"You make your point, Chief of Unit Beauchamp." How carefully had she prepared for this meeting? What was just a one-hour stop-and-admire visit for him had been intense preparation by how many skilled people?

Together they turned back to the window. The temple was a long line of exotic stone buildings stretching half a mile along the crest of the promontory. "They really do look as if they belong to the land."

"Yes, sir, you have a good eye. This is not only an exceptional sample of Khmer Empire architecture, blending to both the stone and the site. It is also a very pure site, culturally. Due to its remote location, it was abandoned for hundreds of years after the fall of the Khmer Empire in the 1400s, preserving the design from future depredation. It has suffered more in the last fifty years than in the five hundred before that."

"What happened fifty years ago?" The chopper circled over the Thai jungle, and he could see what he assumed were Thai Army vehicles stationed along the highway. A dug-in camp lurked farther back in the trees. A glance back revealed that Frank Adams was also observing them very closely.

"The Khmer Rouge, Mr. President." Pok and Moul both looked grim at even the mention of the name of that brutal piece of their country's history. Two million or more had died on the Killing Fields of Pol Pat, a quarter of Cambodia's population. Only Vietnam had stood against him, for which they had been internationally reviled. It was moments like this that made his heart hurt. How could he work to help improve a planet which was capable of such events?

# # #

Genny stayed close by the President as they toured the temple. The helicopters had gone back aloft to provide additional protection. A line of Secret Service agents had secured the entry. Other than a half dozen agents, the two Cambodians, and the dozen news people who had been authorized to join them after an arduous land journey of several hours duration, they were alone.

"You are beautiful. You belong in such places." The President's whisper was barely enough to reach her ears though they stood but a pace apart. Frank was next closest, and appeared to be listening to his radio.

"You are 'deeply enamored' and therefore also deeply biased. It is this place that is so beautiful, Mr. President. It is a sad horror, the things that occur here. This was the last place of resistance against the Khmer Rouge, the last holdout before Pol Pot destroyed this country. It was also the last place the Khmer Rouge held, when Vietnam finally defeated them."

"Well, it is very defensible."

"It is also very steep. It is where in 1979 the Thai government drove forty thousand Cambodian refugees from the Khmer Rouge off the cliff to 'send them home.' Ten thousand died on the descent, or in the mine fields below. This is not a happy place, Mr. President. But it is an important one."

She led him to *Gropura IV.* "There is no building like this one left in the world. It is unique, and now it has been damaged by the gunfire between Cambodia and Thailand."

They stood side-by-side in the knee-high grass and looked up at the temple before them. The gray base rose person-tall in broad horizontal layers of curved and lined stone. It stretched ten meters wide and over fifty long. The roof was long gone, but square columns a meter through reached several stories into the air, holding an equally massive lintel of stone as easily now as it had for a thousand years. At either end of the *gropura* stood a massive crown of carved stone another half-dozen meters tall.

"That such a thing, older than Angkor Wat, should still be standing is a miracle."

"What does it mean?" Peter took her hand.

"You shouldn't do that, Mr. President, we are being watched." But he kept his hand in hers. He had decided they were a couple, and apparently no longer cared what anyone thought. Did she? Not enough to withdraw her hand.

"What does it mean?" he kept his voice even.

She looked around. Pok and Moul were enthralled to have such access to American news services and were making the most of it back at the Second *Gropura*. Only Frank and Beatrice were close to them. Several other Secret Service agents were ranged between them and the rest of their party.

"Preah Vihear was a temple built to Shiva, the Hindu God of Transformation, of Beginnings and Endings. It was a place of worship and meditation. We have also identified those two buildings," she pointed back the structures to either side of *Gropura III,* "as libraries. This was also a place of learning."

"Transformation, you say?"

"Yes." Once again she attempted to recover her hand. "You really should not do this in front of the reporters. It is not seemly for the President to be seen so with a woman to whom he isn't married." She lifted their joined hands and began peeling back his index finger.

"I plan to marry you, Kim-Ly Geneviève Beauchamp, if you'll have me. So, I think the American press will simply have to get used to it."

Genny struggled for a moment longer until his words sunk in.

"You…What?" Her ears were ringing. The vast silence that was Preah Vihear had suddenly been filled with a roar louder than a typhoon upon the ocean that lay five hundred kilometers away. She was suddenly glad for Peter's hand holding hers so that she didn't simply collapse to the ground.

"This is a place of transformation, is it not?"

Genny found a nod somewhere, but her voice was gone.

Peter turned to look at her with those soft warm eyes of his. He took her other hand. Her only anchors in the whirling storm about her, his two strong hands. Then he dropped to one knee before her.

She might have heard Frank Adams in the background say, "Oh shit!" But it was hard to tell.

"Will you have me, Geneviève? I don't know how we will live together, but I know that I cannot stand to live apart."

She made her living with words, with being able to handle and manage any situation. In this moment she had lost any words and could only nod her head and see Peter's answering smile.

Frank Adams shouted something in the background.

Then he tackled her from behind and drove them all to the ground.

Chapter 12

Genny lay dazed for a moment. Had she just agreed to marry the President of the United States? She had. Peter had asked and she'd said yes. Okay, she'd nodded her agreement, but that didn't make it any less true.

Then someone had tackled her.

Frank.

He'd slammed her to the ground.

He rolled off her and now lay on top of Peter. Then Beatrice slammed down onto Genny.

"I wasn't trying to kill your President. I was only saying I marry him. Would marry him," she corrected her English.

She struggled to sit up, shoving at Beatrice, who didn't give way.

"Damn it! Lie still, Ms. Beauchamp!" Beatrice's voice was clipped, hard.

"That's supposed to be Genny…" But she didn't get much energy behind it as she became aware of what else was happening at Temple Preah Vihear.

Gunfire above them.

And, she looked skyward, a green-and-white Marine helicopter spiraling down out of the sky.

Chapter 13

Peter had at least seen Frank barreling toward him a moment before he crashed into them, but it hadn't soften the blow. Geneviève had flailed into him and Frank had driven them both into the grass.

He knew of only one reason Frank would do such a thing.

Sure enough. Gunfire. Up in the air. All the scenarios, all the lectures about domestic crazies and international terrorists did nothing to prepare him for the shock.

Someone was trying to kill him. He didn't know which was worse, the cold fear that swamped him, or the terror that they might kill Geneviève instead.

Even as Frank rolled over to cover him and Beatrice moved in to cover Geneviève, Peter could see at least some of what was happening. One of the escort planes had shot down one of the Marine One choppers. Flames coming out of her engines, the chopper was spiraling down toward the ground, the pilot clearly fighting to perform an auto-rotate landing.

Even as he watched, the second chopper was struck.

The crew chiefs were fighting back with rifles, but were no match for the fighter jet. They were close enough to the ground, that though they pretty much fell out of sky, they didn't have far to fall. Still they rolled and tumbled until they fetched up hard on part of the temple. A huge stone block high atop a column teetered, wobbled, and then settled without falling.

"I've got to move you, now!" Frank grabbed his shoulder and dragged him to his feet.

Geneviève was still struggling to free herself from beneath Beatrice. "She's coming with us."

"No time, Mr. President." Frank pulled at him again but he resisted.

"My fiancée is coming with us!"

"Fiancée?" Frank stared at him nose-to-nose for two heartbeats as he digested the information, his fist still clamped in the shoulder of Peter's suit jacket. "Got it. Beat, up! We're on the move!"

In moments, Peter had Geneviève's hand clamped in his. The two of them stayed low and sprinted behind Frank.

The plane, having finished the choppers, now strafed the people on the plateau, scattering them like chaff.

Frank dove behind a low temple wall. Peter dragged Geneviève down with him as he did the same.

The scattered Secret Service agents returned fire, but handguns and small rifles against a jet served as little more than a distraction to the pilot.

Then the agents grouped together and moved away.

"Hey, shouldn't they be coming to help protect us?"

"Mr. President," Frank had his gun out and was scanning the sky and ground for other attackers. "Per training, they're pretending they already have you with them to draw the aggressor's fire. Now shut up, I'm busy trying to save you."

Sure enough, the plane took another run at the cluster of agents moving toward the entrance of the temple complex.

Frank was calling into his radio. "Merlin unharmed. Continue to distract."

The plane fired a rocket that impacted a low stone wall a hundred feet away, close to the clustered agents. There was a roar that pounded against Peter's ears and a ball of fire. Fragments of rock whistled through the air, he saw two agents drop to the ground.

Then a second plane dove in. It attacked the first.

"He's a renegade!" Peter shouted to Frank. It would fit. One plane doing his job, but the other one hijacked for the attack. Target of opportunity.

Frank nodded, "But why would they want to kill you?"

"They don't." Geneviève crawled up to face Frank. "Injure, perhaps. The pilot could easily have placed that rocket in the center of those agents. I think that the President is wanted alive, as a bargaining chip. The question is by who?"

Peter looked at her. Her hair was a mess, her lip was bleeding, and her hands scraped raw, but she didn't seem to care about that. Instead, she looked pissed, and calculating.

"Cambodians?" Frank was watching the two planes dogfight above, but he was clearly paying attention to what Geneviève had to say.

"No. The President is a guest of their country. You saw how offended Minister Pok was by Thailand's claims to the temple. Nationalist pride. He'd never want to harm the President while he was a guest of Cambodia. Thailand?"

Peter finally saw it.

"Yes, Thailand. And not some random terrorist. This is government sponsored, or at least a faction of it. They hijacked a Cambodian fighter jet to attack us. If he survives the Cambodian jet's attempt to protect us—"

An explosion shattered the air above. A ball of fire exploded just past the edge of the escarpment. A shattered jet spun downward in flames. No pilot ejected.

"Which was that?"

"The Cambodian, sir. One Thai fighter is still aloft."

"Then, if Geneviève is right," Peter kept an eye on the plane. "He will make one or two more runs at us for show, wounding but not killing. After that, he'll be shot down by the Thai Army forces we saw stationed beyond the entrance. But they'll shoot him down over Thai soil so that he has a chance to parachute to safety."

"Then," Geneviève picked up the story. "Then they will come to capture you, killing all of the Cambodians. They will claim that they saved you and use it as an excuse to attack Cambodia, if not in war, then in the international courts."

"Which means," Frank glanced at his watch. "We have about three minutes to get you off this plateau, Mr. President."

"I know the way!" Genny spoke as if she too were one of his trained agents. "But I need a *couteau*. A knife."

Frank looked at her in confusion as she held out a palm.

With a shrug, Frank produced one from somewhere.

Geneviève used it to slit the side of her skirt well up her thigh. She handed the knife back to Frank.

"You own me a new skirt, Mr. President."

"I'll buy you a wedding dress, Geneviève."

She flashed him a smile, then was off and running.

Peter made to follow, but Frank stopped him with a hand against the center of his chest.

Frank stared him straight in the eye. "You trust her?"

"A hundred percent. And she's Southeast Asia Chief of Unit for UNESCO World Heritage. She knows this site better than anyone here."

Frank processed for an eyeblink, then nodded.

Then Peter, Frank, and Beatrice sprinted after Geneviève.

Chapter 14

*T*his is crazy!" *Beatrice* shouted in Genny's ear.

The agent had caught up, but let Genny lead as they dodged through the temple grounds. Now, they were holed up by the water cistern below *Gropura II*. They were twenty meters below the main temple level. She'd worn low-heeled shoes knowing they'd be walking around the site, but wished she'd worn sneakers. She tore the slit in her skirt a little higher, she should have slit both sides.

"The Thai Army is about to storm the entrance," Frank arrived with Peter close beside him. Then he pointed to the north. "And the Cambodian reinforcements are going to be coming up the road to the west. That's where we have to get, but you are leading us down to the east. Why?"

"Because we aren't using either road."

Genny focused on Frank, knowing it was him she had to convince.

"There are a few dozen Cambodian fighters near the entrance gate. They hold the high ground above the entrance stairs. These are veterans, if the Khmer people know anything, it is war. The Thais may be a better equipped, more modern army, but the Khmer will hold their ground for a long time despite being vastly outnumbered."

Frank nodded as he acknowledged her assessment.

"And the nearest reinforcements are probably in Angkor Wat. That's an hour away, even under the very best of conditions, which these roads do not ever have. The nearest air assets are in Phnom Penh, an hour away, if they even are aware of the attack."

"They know. If Beale tells them. I reached her and she's enroute overland."

Genny felt better for that. But overland meant Emily was still in Vietnam and would be at least an hour away.

"We need to keep the President safe from the Thai Army for at least an hour and I know only one way to do that."

She could see Frank weighing factors.

As if on cue, the hijacked Cambodian fighter plane made one more strafing run, this time clearly firing hard on the Cambodian positions at the *Gropura I* entrance. Then, the Cambodian return fire must have scored a hit, as the Thai forces would probably be missing the hijacked plane on purpose, just firing for show. The jet wobbled in the sky as if it had stumbled and tripped, then it caught on fire. Moments later, well into Thailand, the pilot ejected and a white chute opened up almost immediately.

"Bastard!" Beatrice cursed beside her.

"You need to decide now!" Genny ordered Frank and gritted her teeth. She did know what was best.

Frank looked at the President.

"Hell of a woman you chose, Mr. President. Congratulations."

"Thanks, I know."

Chapter 15

*P*eter *followed his* "hell of a woman" as she led his Secret Service detail to the northeast through the trees. They struck down-slope whenever they could, avoiding both the cliff edge and any sight lines to the Thai forces above.

Frank reported that most of his Secret Service squad was joining with the Cambodians in defense of the temple. Only one of the six Marines from the two choppers was uninjured and two were dead.

"You know that the Thais will simply claim it was one renegade Lieutenant or something, gone crazy and acting on his own. When we insist on having the pilot, they will conveniently claim that he was killed trying to escape." Frank's voice was grim.

"Doesn't change where the U.S. will be placing their voice on the international scene. But first, you've got to get me out of this alive."

"Not me. It's up to your girlfriend there."

Genny broke for the next group of trees, sprinting like a gazelle. Her legs, impossibly long, flashing from her skirt, her hair flying behind her like a banner.

"Well, if I'm going to go running after something Frank, it would be hard to find something better than that."

Frank clapped him on the shoulder and they sprinted off together.

Chapter 16

There is a stairway there," Geneviève was pointing at a spot another hundred yards along the escarpment. "Two thousand steps down the cliff face and we will be in Cambodia, far out of the reach of the Thai. Even a parking lot with room for Emily to make her landing."

Peter looked out over the edge of the escarpment. "That's like a two-hundred story building, right?"

"You have better idea on how to save your life?" Suddenly Geneviève displayed a new side to him. This was a woman out at her limits of confidence, terrified that a single mistake could kill them all.

"Anywhere you lead, I'll follow. That's a promise."

She took a deep breath, huffed it out, and nodded once, blinking hard. Geneviève turned to survey the next stretch. "But you should have instead a guarantee made," she added without turning.

"Why?" What was she talking about?

"Guarantee is worth more points." Then she was gone to peek around the next tree. "Bad news as I expect."

"Promise" versus "Guarantee." No. "Promise" was more Scrabble points. Except "Guarantee" would most likely be played off an "an" so it would use all seven tiles. Their lives were at risk and the woman was browbeating him with Scrabble.

He started to sidle up beside her, but Frank shoved him to the ground.

"Two Thai soldiers guard head of stairs." Her syntax was slipping even more than usual under the stress.

"Can't shoot them," Frank observed. "Too long a shot at this distance with a handgun. But, more importantly, we can't have anyone else coming to investigate."

"You three stay here, but be ready in case this doesn't work." Genny pulled off her shoes and took off running in just her stocking feet over the grass and rock.

"What the hell?" Frank moved up to Genny's former position behind the tree, which let Peter move up close beside him.

"Should I?" Beat asked her boss.

"No," Frank shook his head. "She's gotten it right so far."

"Help! Help me!" Genny cried out to the soldiers.

Peter could see her sprinting toward the two guards who had raised their rifles.

She tumbled and fell to the ground.

Peter surged to his feet and it took both Frank and Beat to keep him in place.

Geneviève scrambled back up and kept running toward the guards as if panicked, though now she was weaving and limping.

The guards had lowered their weapons and were moving toward her, perhaps thinking this was one of the hostages they wanted. Little did they know how true that was. But she was now much closer to them. There was no way to help her. What was she thinking?

"Please! Help!" Her cries were softer with distance, but she sounded winded as well. What if she'd broken a rib in her fall or…

Twenty feet from the first guard, she shifted into a clean sprint. At ten feet, she leapt into the air. Even later Peter was never able to fully credit what he saw.

Genny lifted into the air as if jerked aloft by a steel cable from the sky rather than just a leap with strong legs. A heel struck the first soldier's chin so hard that his head snapped back cruelly. She used the gained momentum to wrap her legs around the second soldier's throat in some sort of a scissored headlock flipping him over backwards and smashing him to the ground.

Frank, Beat, and Peter began sprinting to the scene in unison.

Even as they did so, he could see her force her knee up and the soldier went limp.

The first soldier was just sitting up, looking dazedly for his rifle when Frank tackled him from behind.

Peter saw the man's neck twist, then break as he rushed by.

Geneviève still lay with her knees wrapped around the second soldier's throat.

"He's done, honey. You can let go." The man's eyes were open but there was no one left to look out through them.

"No, I can't." Her voice was tight. Thin.

"Are you hurt?" Peter knelt down to check her over.

"No. Not much. But I can't." Tears were starting from her eyes and he didn't know what to do about it.

Frank came up to them, and slowly unwound her legs from around the dead man's neck, pulled her skirt into some semblance of order. Beat dragged the corpse clear then began stripping the two soldiers of their weapons.

Frank squatted down until he was looking right at Geneviève. He wasn't saying anything, just looking at her. In such a rush since the moment that the first chopper had been hit, he'd suddenly gone quiet.

"What was that, anyway?" Peter had never seen anything like it.

"Việt Võ Đạo," Frank said softly not looking up from the silently crying Geneviève. "Flying scissor kick." Then he held a hand out and helped her to her feet.

When she was standing, he nodded once.

"Are you okay to continue?"

She nodded, but clearly couldn't speak.

Peter wrapped an arm around her, she was stiff. So stiff. As if she were made of steel not flesh and blood.

Frank addressed her once more, "Let's all hope you never have to do that outside of the dojo again, but you did it when it counted. And you did it perfectly."

Then he turned to face Peter.

"She just killed a man to save your life. Not many can do that. Even fewer can stand back up afterwards. I can only hope to God that you never have to try it yourself. You take good care of this one, Mr. President, or I'm going to have to hurt you. We clear?"

Peter looked into those dark eyes, and didn't doubt for a second that Frank meant exactly what he said.

Chapter 17

*Y**ou've got to save* me!"

Daniel pretended to hide behind Peter while looking back over the crowd of guests filling the White House State Dining Room. Men in suits, women in elegant gowns. Daniel, as his best man, wore a very smart dark-gray tux which complimented his own black one. Even among the crowd, Peter could easily spot First Lady Kim-Ly Geneviève Matthews, a shining light in the swirl of the people gathered about her.

"What's the problem?" he asked without taking his eyes off the vision before him.

"Genny's sister Jacqi won't leave me alone. Keeps talking about dragging me back to her woman-cave, whatever that is."

Peter dragged his eyes away from his wife to inspect Daniel and squinted at him for a moment.

"You'd make a cute couple."

"You're not helping," Daniel snagged two flutes of champagne from a passing waiter and handed one over.

"She knows you're married, right?"

"Sure, even introduced her to Alice."

"And…"

Daniel took a deep swallow from the narrow flute. "Alice and Jacqi are negotiating using me on a time-share basis."

"Tell Jacqi that three months is my best offer. Can't spare you more than that."

"I'm not a damned condo."

"Sorry, buddy, best I can do. I have to go and be Presidential."

"Meaning you have to go ogle the woman you just married."

"Hard not to."

"Especially in that dress."

Peter didn't bother to reply as he headed into the crowd.

# # #

"Okay if I interrupt?"

Genny couldn't take her eyes off Peter as he approached where she stood with Emily and Gram.

Mrs. Genny Matthews. The sound of it was both intensely foreign and equally perfect. It was a statement of who she had become and where she wanted to be. His black tux and white tie gave him an old world elegance.

"No," Em shook her head. "She's ours. She'll be yours the rest of your lives. We get her a while longer."

Peter slid a hand around Genny's waist, pulling her tight beside him. He kissed her on the temple and whispered in her ear, "I love you."

She melted every time he said that.

"Easy there," Emily teased Genny's husband. "The night's still young and she looks too perfect. No mussing her up yet, Sneaker Boy."

"Sneaker Boy?" It was like a galvanic shock coursing through her body.

"Sure," Emily nodded toward the man even now threatening to undo Genny's hair from the elegant coif atop her head. "Tossed him in the Reflecting Pool out on the Washington Mall ages ago. All he could do was whine about his sneakers getting all wet."

"Wet and muddy," Peter clarified as if in his own defense. "And she didn't mention that they were brand new, too."

"Sneaker Boy?" Genny knew she was repeating herself, but it was really too perfect. It started as a smile, but it turned to a giggle. A high one that she just couldn't stop. Not until she had laughed until she cried and gotten wet spots all over Peter's lapel when she hugged him, could she finally speak.

They were all looking at her strangely. Smiles on their faces even though they didn't know why.

"Gram, you remember the one I told you about, on the computer?"

"Yes. The one who plays such good games." Her grandmother smiled as if she'd known all along. As if there was no question that the world worked this way.

"Do you want to tell my husband what our shared name means?"

"Well, if you are Sneaker Boy, of course you had to marry Kim-Ly." Then Gram poked Genny's new husband in the ribs to emphasize the joke. "Our name means Golden Lion."

Peter simply looked stunned. "All of those games we played on-line at the Scrabble site, and you are the Golden Lion?"

"It fits her does it not?" Gram suddenly glared at him and he blanched.

"It's perfect. Just as she is. Perfect."

Gram nodded as if making sure he understood that last point clearly.

# # #

Peter kept nuzzling Genny's neck as they danced around the State Dining Room floor. Though it was a warm day in June, it was their first dance as a couple after all, Peter had made them play a Christmas carol.

"It is the wrong carol," she told him though she didn't really care. "This is not the first one that we danced to."

"I couldn't remember what it was. I could only remember the first time I held you in my arms."

She kept her head on his shoulder and let him tease her. It had been such a perfect day. They had married where they met, out by the National Christmas Tree, now just a tall spruce awaiting next year's decorations. It was a huge affair that had drawn an astonishing crowd of well-wishers. A near-death experience had made the President even more popular.

In Thailand, a right-wing faction had been stripped of all power, the left using the excuse of the trumped-up attack to perform a major housecleaning of the ranks. Maybe now there was a chance for peace at Preah Vihear.

Tomorrow, she would go to her office in the East Wing.

Despite Peter's offers of a role in the Department of the Interior, she had decided to stay with UNESCO. The Director had created a position specifically for her. World Heritage Convention Ambassador to the U.N. Her mandate, to be an advocate for the Heritage Sites with the hundred-and-ninety three member nations' Ambassadors.

The First Lady's office had been converted to a tech center that would let her reach around the world, flying an hour to New York only when essential meetings occurred.

Maybe when Peter retired, they would move to New York or perhaps Paris, so that she could be near the UNESCO headquarters.

For now, she simply let herself float in the arms of the man she loved.

"I'm not sure how much longer I can stand it, until I get you out of that incredible dress."

She knew exactly how he felt. Peter looked so glorious in his tux.

"Well, Mr. President husband, there is only one way that is going to happen."

"What? If I deport everyone in the room?"

"No." She looked up into those dreamy eyes and kissed him as they danced. She could hear the cameras snapping away and simply didn't care. She was too happy.

"No. The only way the President of the United States will get the First Lady of the United States out of her dress, is if they are standing in the middle of the Oval Office."

She rested her head back on his shoulder as he groaned quietly.

Yes, a perfect day indeed.

About the Author

M. *L. Buchman, in* among his career as a corporate project manager, he has rebuilt and single-handed a fifty-foot sailboat, both flown and jumped out of airplanes, designed and built two houses, and bicycled solo around the world. His romances, as M.L. Buchman, have been named "NPR Top 5 Romance of the Year" and "Booklist Top 10 Romance of the Year." He is now making his living full-time as a writer, living on the Oregon Coast. He is constantly amazed at what you can do with a degree in Geophysics. Please keep up with his writing at www.mlbuchman.com.

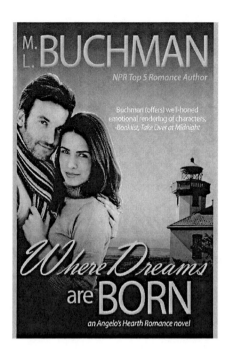

Where Dreams Are Born (excerpt)

*R*ussell *locked his door* as the last of the staff finally went home and turned off his camera.

He knew it was good. The images were there, solid. He'd really captured them.

But something was missing.

The groove ran so clean when he slid into it. The studio faded into the background, then the strobe lights, reflector umbrellas, and blue and green backdrops all became texture and tone.

Image, camera, man became one and they were all that mattered; a single flow of light beginning before time was counted and ending in the printed image. A ray of primordial light traveling forever to glisten off the BMW roadster still parked in one corner of the wood-planked studio. Another ray lost in the dark blackness of the finest leather bucket seats. One more picking out the supermodel's perfect hand dangling a single, shining, golden key. The image shot just slow enough that they key blurred as it spun, but the logo remained clear.

He couldn't quite put his finger on it…

Another great ad by Russell Morgan. Russell Morgan, Inc. The client would be knocked dead, and the ad leaving all others standing still as it roared down the passing lane. Might get him another Clio, or even a second Mobius.

But… There wasn't usually a "but." The groove had definitely been there, but he hadn't been in it. That was the problem. It had slid along, sweeping his staff into their own orchestrated perfection, but he'd remained untouched. Not part of that ideal, seamless flow.

"Be honest, boyo, that session sucked," he told the empty studio. Everything had come together so perfectly for yet another ad for yet another high-end glossy. *Man, the Magazine* would launch spectacularly in a few weeks, a high-profile mid-December launch, a never before seen twelve page spread by Russell Morgan, Inc. and the rag would probably never pay off the lavish launch party of hope, ice sculptures, and chilled magnums of champagne before disappearing like a thousand before it.

He stowed the last camera he'd been using with the others piled by his computer. At the breaker box he shut off the umbrellas, spots, scoops, and washes. The studio shifted from a stark landscape in hard-edged relief to a nest of curious shadows and rounded forms. The tang of hot metal and deodorant were the only lasting result of the day's efforts.

"Morose tonight, aren't we?" he asked his reflection in the darkened window of his Manhattan studio. His reflection was wise enough to not answer back. There wasn't ever a "down" after a shoot, there had always been an "up."

Not tonight.

He'd kept everyone late, even though it was Thanksgiving eve, hoping for that smooth slide of image, camera, man. It was only when he saw the power of the images he captured that he knew he wasn't a part of the chain anymore and decided he'd paid enough triple-time expenses.

The single perfect leg wrapped in thigh-high red-leather boots visible in the driver's seat. The sensual juxtaposition of woman and sleek machine. An ad designed to wrap every person with even a hint of a Y-chromosome around its little finger. And those with only X-chromosomes would simply want to be her. A perfect combo of sex for the guys and power for the women.

Russell had become no more than the observer, the technician behind the camera. Now that he faced it, months, maybe even a year had passed since he'd been yanked all the way into the light-image-camera-man slipstream. Tonight was the first time he hadn't even trailed in the churned up wake.

"You're just a creative cog in the advertising photography machine." Ouch! That one stung, but it didn't turn aside the relentless steamroller of his thoughts speeding down some empty, godforsaken autobahn.

His career was roaring ahead, his business fast and smooth, but, now that he considered it, he really didn't give a damn.

His life looked perfect, but—"Don't think it!" —but his autobahn mind finished, "it wasn't."

Russell left his silent reflection to its own thoughts and went through the back door that led to his apartment, closing it tightly on the perfect BMW, the perfect rose on the seat, and somewhere, lost among a hundred other props from dozens of other shoots, the long pair of perfect red-leather Chanel boots that had been wrapped around the most expensive legs in Manhattan. He didn't care if he never walked back through that door again. He'd been doing his art by rote, and how God-awful sad was that?

And he shot commercial art. He'd never had the patience to do art for art's sake. No draw for him. No fire. He left the apartment dark, only a soft glow from the blind-covered windows revealing the vaguest outlines of the framed art on the wall. Even that almost overwhelmed him.

He didn't want to see the huge prints by the art artists: autographed Goldsworthy, Liebowitz, and Joseph Francis' photomosaics for the moderns. A hundred and fifty more rare, even one of a kind prints, all the way back through Bourke-White to his prize, an original Daguerre. The collection that the Museum of Modern Art kept begging to borrow for a show. He bypassed the circle of chairs and sofas that could be a playpen for two or a party for twenty. He cracked the fridge in the stainless steel and black kitchen searching for something other than his usual beer.

A bottle of Krug.

Maybe he was just being grouchy after a long day's work.

Milk.

No. He'd run his enthusiasm into the ground but good.

Juice even.

Would he miss the camera if he never picked it up again?

No reaction.

Nothing.

Not even a twinge.

That was an emptiness he did not want to face. Alone, in his apartment, in the middle of the world's most vibrant city.

Russell turned away, and just as the door swung closed, the last sliver of light, the relentless cold blue-white of the refrigerator bulb, shone across his bed. A quick grab snagged the edge of the door and left the narrow beam illuminating a long pale form on his black bedspread.

The Chanel boots weren't in the studio. They were still wrapped around those three thousand dollar-an-hour legs. The only clothing on a perfect body, five foot-eleven of intensely toned female anatomy, right down to her exquisitely stair-mastered behind. Her long, white-blond hair, a perfect Godiva over the tanned breasts. Except for their too exact symmetry, even the closest inspection didn't reveal the work done there. One leg raised just ever so slightly to hide what was meant to be revealed later. Discovered.

Melanie.

By the steady rise and fall of her flat stomach, he knew she'd fallen asleep, waiting for him to finish in the studio.

How long had they been an item? Two months? Three?

She'd made him feel alive. At least when he was with her. The image of the supermodel in his bed. On his arm at yet another SoHo gallery opening, dazzling New York's finest at another three-star restaurant, wooing another gathering of upscale people with her ever so soft, so sensual, so studied French accent. Together they were wired into the heart of the in-crowd.

But that wasn't him, was it? It didn't sound anything like the Russell he once knew.

Perhaps "they" were about how he looked on her arm?

Did she know tomorrow was the annual Thanksgiving ordeal at his parents? That he'd rather die than attend? Any number of eligible woman floating about who'd finagled an invitation in hopes of snaring one of *People Magazine*'s "100 Most Eligible." Heir to a billion or some such, but wealthy enough on his own, by his own sweat. Number twenty-four this year, up from forty-seven the year before despite Tom Cruise being available yet again.

No.

Not Melanie. It wasn't the money that drew her. She wanted him. But more, she wanted the life that came with him, wrapped in the man package. She wanted The Life. The one that People Magazine readers dreamed about between glossy pages.

His fingertips were growing cold where they held the refrigerator door cracked open.

If he woke her there'd be amazing sex. Or a great party to go to. Or...

Did he want "Or"? Did he want more from her? Sex. Companionship. An energy, a vivacity, a thirst he feared that he lacked. Yes.

But where hid that smooth synchronicity like light-image-cameraman? Where lurked that perfect flow from one person to another? Did she feel it? Could he... ever again?

"More?" he whispered into the darkness to test the sound.

The door slid shut, escaped from numb fingers, plunging the apartment back into darkness, taking Melanie along with it.

His breath echoed in the vast darkness. Proof that he was alive, if nothing more.

Time to close the studio. Time to be done with Russell Incorporated. Then what?

Maybe Angelo would know what to do. He always claimed he did. Maybe this time Russell would actually listen to his almost-brother, though he knew from the experience of being himself for the last thirty years that was unlikely. Seattle. Damn! He'd have to go to bloody Seattle to find his best friend.

He could guarantee that wouldn't be a big hit with Melanie.

Now if he only knew if that was a good thing or bad.

# # #

JANUARY 1

If you were still alive, you'd pay for this one, Daddy." The moment the words escaped her lips, Cassidy Knowles slapped a hand over her mouth to negate them, but it was too late.

The sharp wind took her words and threw them back into the pine trees, guilt and all. It might have stopped her, if it didn't make this the hundredth time she'd cursed him this morning.

She leaned into the wind and forged her way downhill until the muddy path broke free from the mossy smell of the trees. Her Stuart Weitzman boots were long since soaked through, and now her feet were freezing. The two-inch heels had nearly flipped her into the mud a dozen different times.

Cassidy Knowles stared at the lighthouse. It perched upon a point of rock, tall and white, with its red roof as straight and snug as a prim bonnet. A narrow trail traced along the top of the breakwater leading to the lighthouse. The parking lot, much to her chagrin, was empty; six, beautiful, empty spaces.

"Sorry, ma'am," park rangers were always polite when telling you what you couldn't do. "The parking lot by the light is reserved for physically-challenged visitors only. You'll have to park here. It is just a short walk to the lighthouse."

The fact that she was dressed for a nice afternoon lunch at Pike Place Market safe in Seattle's downtown rather than a blustery mile-long walk on the first day of the year didn't phase the ranger in the slightest.

Cassidy should have gone home, would have, if it hadn't been for the letter stuffed deep in her pocket. So, instead of a tasty treat in a cozy deli, she'd buttoned the top button of her suede Bernardo jacket and headed down the trail. At least the promised rain had yet to arrive, so the jacket was only cold, not wet. The stylish cut had never been intended to fight off the bajillion mile-an-hour gusts that snapped it painfully against her legs. And her black leggings ranged about five layers short of tolerable and a far, far cry from warm.

At the lighthouse, any part of her that had been merely numb slipped right over to quick frozen. Leaning into the wind to stay upright, tears streaming from her eyes, she could think of a thing or two to tell her father despite his recent demise and her general feelings about the usefulness of upbraiding a dead man.

"What a stupid present!" the wind tore her shout word-by-word, syllable-by-syllable and sent flying back toward her nice warm car and the smug park ranger.

A calendar.

He'd given her a stupid calendar of stupid lighthouses and a stupid letter to open at each stupid one. He'd been very insistent, made her promise. One she couldn't ignore. A deathbed promise.

Cassidy leaned grimly forward to start walking only to have the wind abruptly cease. She staggered, nearly planting her face on the pavement before another gust sent her crabbing sideways. With resolute force, she planted one foot after another until she'd crossed that absolutely vacant parking lot with its six empty spaces and staggered along the top of the breakwater to reach the lighthouse itself. No handicapped people crazy enough to come here New Year's morning. No people at all for that matter.

The building's wall was concrete, worn smooth by a thousand storms and a hundred coats of brilliant white paint. With the wind practically pinning her to the outside of the building, she peeked into one of the windows. The wind blew her hair about so that it beat on her eyes and mouth trying to simultaneously blind and choke her. With one hand, she grabbed the unruly mass mostly to one side. With the other she shaded the dusty window. The cobwebbed glass revealed an equally unkempt interior.

No lightkeeper sitting in his rocking chair before a merry fire. No smoking pipe. No lighthouse cat curled in his lap. Some sort of a rusty engine not attached to anything. A bucket of old tools. A couple of paint cans.

A high wave crashed into the rocks with a thundering shudder that ran up through the heels of her boots and whipped a chill spray into the wind. Salt water on suede.

Daddy now owed her a new coat as well.

Cassidy edged along the foundation until she found a calmer spot, a bit of windshadow behind the lighthouse where the wind chill ranked merely miserable rather than horrific on the suck-o-meter. Squatting down behind one of the breakwater's boulders helped a tiny bit more. She peeled off her thin leather gloves and blew against her fingertips to warm them enough so that they'd work. Once she'd regained some modicum of feeling, she pulled out the letter.

She couldn't feel his writing, though she ran her fingertips over it again and again. His Christmas present. A five-dollar calendar of Washington lighthouses from the hospital gift store and a dozen thin envelopes wrapped in an old x-ray folder, god, the x-ray folder, with no ribbon, no paper.

In the end he'd foiled her final Christmas hunt. It had been her great yearly quest. The ultimate grail of childhood, finding the key present before Christmas morning. There was no present he could hide that she couldn't find. Not the Cabbage Patch Kid when she was six; the one she'd had to hold with her arm in a cast, from falling off the kitchen stool she'd dragged into her father's closet. Not the used VW Rabbit he'd hidden out in the wine shed thinking that she never went there anymore. And she didn't, except for some reason the day before her eighteenth Christmas.

A part of her wanted to crumple the letter up and throw it into the sea. It was too soon. She didn't want to face the pain again.

Too soon.

The rest of her did what it supposed to do.

The dutiful daughter opened the envelope and pinned the letter against her thigh so that she could read the slashing scrawl that was her father's. Even as weak with sickness as he must have been, it looked scribed in stone. His bold-stroke writing gave the words a force and strength just as his deep voice had once sounded strong enough to keep the world at bay for his small girl.

Dearest Ice Sweet,

He'd always called her that.

Icewine. The grapes traditionally harvested on her birthday, December twenty-first. "The sweetest wine of all, my little ice sweet girl." By the age of five she knew about the sugar content of icewine, Riesling, Chardonnay, and a dozen others. By eight she could identify scores of vintages just by the scent of the cork and hundreds by their logos though she'd yet to taste more than thimblefuls of watered wine at any one time.

Cassidy stared at the waves digging angrily at the rocks. Spray slashed sideways by the wind dragged tears from her eyes even as she struggled to blink them dry. She hadn't cried in a long time and she was damned if she was going to start now simply because she was cold and there was a hole in her heart.

Seven days. She'd looked away for a one moment seven days ago and he was gone. Christmas morning. He'd hung on long enough to tell her of his last present, hidden in plain sight in the used X-ray folder on the side table. A long list of crossed-out names had shuttled films back and forth across Northwest Hospital. Last used by someone named Barash. No meaning for her whatsoever.

> *I bought this calendar the day you moved back to Seattle.*
> *Marked in all the "dates." Now I know that I won't get*
> *to go with you. I'm sorry to leave you so young.*

"I'm twenty-nine, Daddy." But it felt young. Her birthday gone unremarked because he'd never woken that day so close to his last. The hole in her heart was so broad that it would never be filled.

He'd only been gone a week. Cremated, waked, and ashes spread on his beloved vineyard by the permission of the new owners. They'd owned his vineyard for five years, but still, they were the new ones. It still wasn't right, them living in the place where her father belonged. She could still picture him striding among the vines, rubbing the soil in his palm, showing his only child the wonders of the changing seasons, the lifecycle of a grapevine, and the nurturing of honeybees.

> *For our first "date" I will just tell you how proud I am of*
> *you. My daughter took a vintner's education and turned*
> *herself into the best food-and-wine columnist ever.*

He always believed in her. Always rooted for her. Always cheered her on. He'd been the same way with her boyfriends. Always welcoming them when they arrived. Always consoling her when they were gone. No judgment, not even on the ones she should have avoided like a bottle of rotgut Thunderbird.

The wind rattled the paper sharply, drawing her attention back to the letter.

> *You are so like me. You figure out what feels right and*
> *you just go do it, damn the consequences. I could never*

fault you for leaving. I always did what I wanted, too. Saw it and went right for it, no discussion needed. All the while wearing perfect blinders that blocked out everything else. You got that from me. You come by your whimsical stubbornness honestly, Ice Sweet.

She wasn't stubborn, years of careful planning had led her this far. Even her move to Seattle to be with him had been calculated, though she never told him about that. She shifted on the hard rock that was in imminent danger of freezing her butt.

Her father kept apologizing for all the wrong things. Seattle had ended up being a great career move, or was becoming one as she'd hoped. In New York, she had worked as one of a thousand food and wine reviewers. Okay one in fifty, maybe even one in twenty-five, she was damn good, but there were only three women at that level. The other twenty-two were members of longstanding in the old boys' club.

"We're looking for someone with a more refined palate." Read as someone who was "male."

She'd let go of her sublet in Manhattan when she'd found out he was sick. Bought a condo in Seattle to be near, but not too near him on Bainbridge Island. Helped him move into the elder-care by Northgate when he couldn't care for himself any longer, and from there to Northwest Hospital where she'd lived out his last two weeks in the chair by his bed.

The *Village Voice* dropped her the day she left Manhattan. That had hurt as they'd run her first-ever review, a short piece on Jim and Charlie's Punk and Wine Bistro. Jim and Charlie's was still there, partly thanks to that review that was still framed and hung in the center of the bar's mirror.

But in Seattle she was rapidly rising to the very upper crust of the apple pie. Her reviews ran in every local paper. The *San Francisco Chronicle* had picked her up for their Travel section the following week making it difficult to stay grumpy about the loss of The Voice. Then AAA took her national with their magazines. From there, it hadn't been a big step to national syndication. Six more months in New York and she'd have still been grinding her way up from the twentieth spot to the nineteenth. She was going to bypass the lot of them by skipping right past the de rigueur hurdles and sitting at the head table herself.

Her father's cancer had brought at least that much good. Now if only it hadn't taken him with it.

And she wasn't whimsical, no matter what he thought. Her dad had always described her mother as the organized one. And Cassidy had done her best to be just like her. You didn't become a topcolumnist by following the wind all willy-nilly.

If she didn't hurry, she was going to freeze in place. She chafed at her legs with one hand and then the other, but it didn't help. She was cold past any cure less than a piping-hot tub bath. She peeked ahead, just two and a bit pages. She turned to the second sheet.

> *I started the vineyard after my tour in Vietnam. Got signed off the base and walked out of San Francisco right across the Golden Gate. No home, no job, no one to go back to. Headed up into the hills, don't even know why or where I was. Walked and hitched 'til dark, slept, woke with the light, and kept moving.*

> *One morning, I woke up in a field, leaning against a rotting, wooden fencepost, looking at the saddest little vineyard you could imagine. Poor vines dying of thirst. I found an old bucket and started watering them from a nearby stream. Old man came out to lean on the fence. Watched me quite a while, a couple hours maybe. I didn't care about him. Those vines were the first thing I'd cared about in a long, long time.*

> *"You want 'em?" the old guy asked. "Five hundred bucks and they're yours."*

> *I don't even remember how it happened. One minute my final pay was in my pocket, then his. Other vets drifted in. I charged them fifty bucks to join. Five of us worked the land, recovered the vines. That was the start of the thirty acres of Knowles Valley Vineyard.*

She'd never heard how his first vineyard started. Didn't even really know where it was, somewhere in the hills of northern California.

Though he might have ambled all the way to Oregon for how much she knew.

> *Walk the year with me. Let's take our time. My past is mine, but your future is not. That's only up to you. I leave you to walk alone, it is a rough trail often over rocky soil. But keep your head high and you'll go far.*
>
> *Whatever happens, know that I love you. I'm so proud of you.*
>
> *Love you Ice Sweet,*
>
> *Vic*

Vic. He always signed his letters "Vic." Never what she'd always called him. "Daddy."

"I could never fault you for leaving." Yet between the lines that's just what he did. Nothing on the backs of any of the pages. She worked to refold the pages in the wind.

"No, you're imagining things, Cass. You think too much. Get your head out of your own butt." And she mostly did. One of the many gifts Vic Knowles had given her, the ability to be clear about her own actions and reactions.

He'd financed her dreams of getting away from the rain capital of the Pacific Northwest. He'd paid for her college in full and cooking school after that. It was only cleaning up his papers this last week that she saw how close it had come to breaking him. He'd just made it a natural assumption that she'd go to college and he'd pay. Just like her Mom who had a degree in economics from Vassar. He'd always talked about how smart Cassidy's mother was. How beautiful. How much he missed her.

He hadn't gone to college himself, not even high school. His past was little more than a few facts she'd winnowed over the years. His dad had left before he could remember. He'd dropped out of third grade to help his mother run the grocery store. They were desperately poor when she died. Then he'd gone to Vietnam at eighteen as the only way to make a living wage. And walked to a vineyard. But he gave Cassidy that gift of education as if it was no sacrifice to him.

Did he now begrudge her that past? The future he never had.

No. That didn't make any sense. He hadn't thought about the money, he'd invested in his dreams for her. She was just going nuts from missing him so much and angry at him for being dead.

"Useful, Cass, real useful."

To prove her sanity, she forced the rumpled letter back into the envelope, as neatly as possible in the midst of the maelstrom, and she forced that back into her leather pack.

Her father, the self-educated man, also the most well-read man she'd ever met. But she'd learned early on to do her math and science homework before he came home from the fields. His frustration at being unable to help her with them had always been a strain.

Cassidy's mother was a single solitary memory. She'd been standing in the open doorway of the house, leaving on a stormy night to answer a call to the hospital. The wind at the door blew her hair across her face as she leaned on her father's arm. Cassidy's only memory of Adrianne Knowles, a woman with no face. Then Bea Clark rushing in from next door to sit with her.

She and Daddy did talk about the books though. He had sharpened her mind as they puzzled out the books together. Ayn Rand piled next to Shakespeare, Heinlein and Hugo, Dickens and a biography of Jimi Hendrix. Their house was always awash in books. And the massive collection of wine books, thumbed again and again by both of them, the only books to have a proper bookcase, had sat in the place of honor in the living room. Everything else jumbled into stacked wooden crates, mounded on tops of dressers, and enough on the dining table to make it a battle to find room for two plates.

The chill spray of a particularly large wave spattered her with a few drops and the next with a few more.

The tide must be coming in.

She scrambled from her hiding place and rose back into the wind which threatened to topple her down into the roaring waves. She forged her way back up the hill. The wind tore at her backpack and thumped it against her spine. The camera. Right.

She squatted to get out of the wind and pulled out her trusty point-and-shoot. The wind nearly blinded her when she turned back into it. Her hair swirled about her head.

A sailboat.

Two lunatics in a sailboat were off the point of land. A cobalt-blue hull climbed out of one wave, pointing its bow to the sky, and then plunged down and buried its nose in the front of the next wave before rising again in a great arc of spray and green water. Huge, maroon sails snapped in the wind, loud enough to sound like a gunshot above the roaring surf.

Whoever the captain was, he and his buddy were crazy. They must both be male because no woman in her right mind would ever go out into a storm like this. But if they wanted to sail right into her picture, she wasn't going to complain; it was a beautiful boat. At the perfect moment she snapped the photo then turned for the woods and the long trail home.

Other Romances by this Author

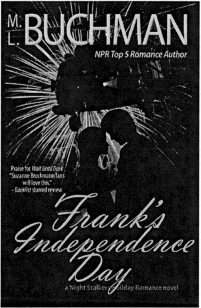

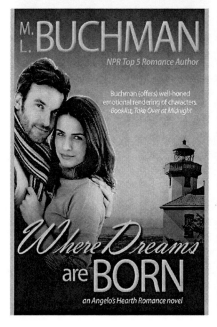

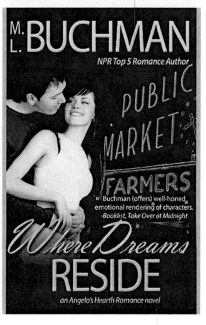

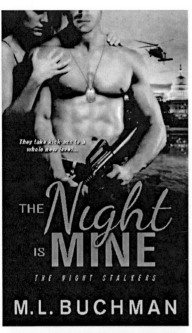

They take kick-ass to a
whole new level...

THE Night
IS MINE

THE NIGHT STALKERS

M.L. BUCHMAN

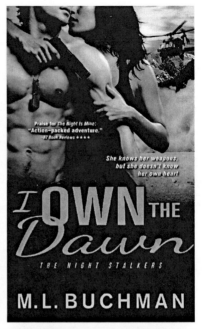

Praise for *The Night Is Mine*:
"Action-packed adventure."
RT Book Reviews ★★★★

She knows her weapons,
but she doesn't know
her own heart

I OWN THE
Dawn

THE NIGHT STALKERS

M.L. BUCHMAN

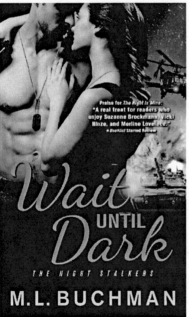

Praise for *The Night Is Mine*:
"A real treat for readers who
enjoy Suzanne Brockmann, Vicki
Hinze, and Merline Lovelace."
★ *Booklist* Starred Review

Wait
UNTIL
Dark

THE NIGHT STALKERS

M.L. BUCHMAN

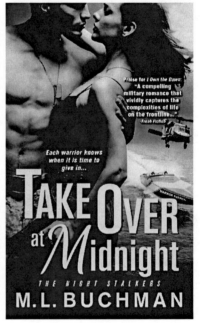

Praise for *I Own the Dawn*:
"A compelling
military romance that
vividly captures the
complexities of life
on the frontline..."
Fresh Fiction

Each warrior knows
when it is time to
give in...

TAKE OVER
at Midnight

THE NIGHT STALKERS

M.L. BUCHMAN

Other fine books by this author

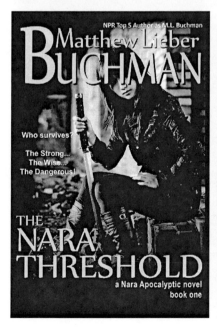

Matthew Lieber

BUCHMAN

When God cheats
at Scrabble, does
Hell freeze over?

Cookbook
from Hell:
Reheated

a Deities Anonymous novel

Matthew Lieber

BUCHMAN

When the Software that Runs
the Universe launches the
Armageddeon subroutine...

Saviors 101:
the first book of the
Reluctant Messiah

a Deities Anonymous novel

CPSIA information can be obtained at www.ICGtesting.com
Printed in the USA
BVOW07s1659150714

359261BV00001B/99/P

9 781492 757283